KURT

The K9 Files, Book 12

Dale Mayer

KURT: THE K9 FILES, BOOK 12
Dale Mayer
Valley Publishing Ltd.

Copyright © 2020

All rights reserved. Except for use in any review, the reproduction or utilization of this work in whole or in part by any electronic, mechanical or other means, now known or hereafter invented, including xerography, photocopying and recording, or in any information storage or retrieval system, is forbidden without the written permission of the publisher.

This is a work of fiction. Names, characters, places, brands, media, and incidents are either the product of the author's imagination or are used fictitiously. Any resemblance to actual events, locales, or persons, living or dead, is entirely coincidental.

ISBN-13: 978-1-773363-18-9
Print Edition

Books in This Series:

Ethan, Book 1
Pierce, Book 2
Zane, Book 3
Blaze, Book 4
Lucas, Book 5
Parker, Book 6
Carter, Book 7
Weston, Book 8
Greyson, Book 9
Rowan, Book 10
Caleb, Book 11
Kurt, Book 12
Tucker, Book 13
Harley, Book 14

About This Book

Welcome to the all new K9 Files series reconnecting readers with the unforgettable men from SEALs of Steel in a new series of action packed, page turning romantic suspense that fans have come to expect from USA TODAY Bestselling author Dale Mayer. Pssst… you'll meet other favorite characters from SEALs of Honor and Heroes for Hire too!

Being a badass growing up had been fine for a while, but Kurt knew his life had to change. His best option? The US Navy. Thirteen years later a serendipitous request from Badger to check out reports of a missing War Dog hidden in the bushes and attacking people sends Kurt to the very place he couldn't wait to get out of.

When Kurt chose the navy over Laurie Ann so long ago, he left her with a gift she'd fought long and hard to keep. Plus she didn't give up on her dream of becoming a doctor. When Kurt returns, it's hard not to see the same person she'd loved in this older version. Yet the town has a long memory, and at least one person isn't willing to see who Kurt is now.

But, as always, he's a trouble magnet. Was he capable of handling the nightmare they were in, or would he leave, just like he had last time?

Sign up to be notified of all Dale's releases here!
https://smarturl.it/DaleNews

PROLOGUE

Kurt Manchester walked into Badger's office. "Wow," he said. "I don't know what to do with this. You have an office of your own."

Badger looked up, grinned, and said, "Kat insisted. Otherwise I leave my shit everywhere."

Kurt laughed, sat down in the guest chair, and said, "What did you want to see me about?"

"I'm sure you've heard about the dogs we've been dealing with," he said, one eyebrow lifted as he looked at Kurt.

Kurt nodded. "Yeah, heard something about it. You're almost done with those, aren't you?"

"Nope, not happening apparently," he said. "We've got another half-dozen here anyway. I haven't even counted but was trying to finish off the original twelve files. And this is the last of them," he said. "When the department went to check on the War Dog, the adoptees admitted that they had only done the adoption for their brother because he'd really, really wanted it. But, when they followed up with the brother, he had taken off, and the dog was nowhere to be found."

"And the problem with that is?"

"We found the brother later. He's in jail."

"Wow," he said. "So where the hell is the dog?"

"The brother has no idea, says that the dog never adjusted well to being there, and wasn't exactly friendly, so he didn't really give a shit."

"Great."

"Yep. Lost in Kentucky."

"Okay," Kurt said, slowly getting an idea. "And that's why you're asking me?"

"Kentucky is your home state, isn't it?"

"Yes," he said. "But how long ago was the dog lost there?"

"Well, we were given the file awhile ago," he said. "And we did look at all these, and absolutely no good leads existed on any of them. So we weren't in too much of a panic to set too many man-hours in this direction. We've done the best we can, but this is the oldest one we've got."

"So that's a really cold case for me to look after," he said, reaching for the file. He opened it up to see a completely golden not-quite-shepherd-looking Malinois. "Female?" he asked from the size.

"Yes, she's female, and, of course, she's fixed. She was an excellent War Dog. She was an IED-sniffing, bomb-sniffing War Dog, and she was really good at sniffing out the enemy in hidden corners. She's an expert at hiding herself and has done a ton of outdoor training. Her name is Sabine."

"In other words, she'll see the world as her enemy. She won't know who to trust, and she has spent all these weeks living on her own."

"Maybe," he said, "and I know you think the department was derelict in not getting to this earlier, but we did contact several people we know throughout the state of Kentucky, and yesterday we got a tip, saying that somebody had seen a dog looking just like this one at a local truck stop."

"Is it likely she's still there?"

"The only thing we could think of is it's the last place that she had human contact. And remember that she's five and that she's spent quite a bit of time with people."

"And was the tip a good tip or a bad tip?"

"That's where the problem comes in," he said. "The tipster said that Sabine was trying to attack people. They'd called animal control, but so far nobody had seen Sabine since."

"I'm on my way," he said, jumping to his feet.

"Wait," Badger said. "We can't pay for this. We'll cover your expenses, but there are no wages."

"That's fine," he said. "Any dog that's been through military training deserves to have a few good years. It sounds like she's been given a short shrift this time."

"It happens," Badger said, "hopefully not too often. The thing is, do you have any K9 training?"

"Maybe not like you mean," he said, "but I've certainly been around dogs all my life. My biological dad bred them. When he was sober that is. My foster families usually had them, for easier assimilation, yada, yada."

"Good enough," he said. "This one could be dangerous."

"She could be." Kurt shrugged. "Yet maybe it's about time somebody went intending to rescue her," he said, "instead of capturing her." And, with that, Kurt walked out.

CHAPTER 1

As Kurt stepped out of the Lexington airport into the bright sunshine, he stopped and took several slow deep breaths. It might have been the area that he grew up in, but it wasn't an area that he had very good memories of. His childhood had been rough; in his teen years, he had bounced off the law more than playing within it. Only as he finally went into the navy did everything improve tremendously. He'd learned discipline and growth. He'd learned what brotherhood was and what it meant to have people who were there for him and who wanted to help him. He'd been very wild and unruly; going into the navy had been the best thing he could have done. School was hit-and-miss for him, and he was not sure if he would graduate because he'd skipped so much school. But somehow he'd squeaked his way all the way through to becoming a Navy SEAL, and the rest was history.

Until his accident.

He'd spent thirteen years in the navy, with his last year in a hospital, but the previous twelve years as a Navy SEAL. The highlight of his career.

He'd been in a freak underwater diving accident, where part of a wreck came down on him. Everybody said it was a total accident and could have happened to anybody at any time. But the fact was, it had happened to him. He looked down at his prosthetic lower right leg and gave it a shake. It always felt weird to think that this mechanical piece was attached to his body now. It was okay, but it just wasn't the same as what it had been before. But he'd long ago given up on feeling sorry for himself. He was alive. He'd almost drowned and then almost hadn't survived the accident. It was pretty hard to imagine a wake-up call with any less of a head smack, saying, *Hey, what's next in your life?*

He shook his head, walked toward the car rental office to pick up the truck he'd ordered. He knew a lot of people would laugh at his choice of a truck. In this case, a large dog was involved, so Kurt needed some space. He also didn't know what he was up against. With that in mind, he headed out for supplies at a pet store.

Once inside, he saw a crate and contemplated it. But he decided that, if and when he was successful in recovering this War Dog, the cage was something that he could use for transporting the dog. In the meantime, it wasn't necessary. At least he hoped not.

With all that on his mind, he walked into the strip mall at the end of the block, picked up a couple sandwiches from a corner deli and a coffee. With those, he headed back out to the street and into the truck. He stopped beside his vehicle to figure out with his cell's GPS exactly where he was going and determined the truck stop was about twenty miles away. He hopped into the vehicle and headed in the direction he needed to go.

He couldn't imagine why the dog would be hanging around the same area, unless something was keeping her there. Animals were fairly simple in that they had basic needs and were usually easy to understand. But the conflicting reports that Badger had been getting from various people wasn't good. It also could mean that the dog was no longer around, if it had truly gotten vicious.

It didn't take much for the locals to turn around and pop an animal like that to ensure that it became a nonissue before it ever got bad. He understood that sentiment in theory, but, at the same time, it was hard on the animals because they didn't get themselves into that situation on their own. Human intervention had picked up this poor female and put her into this crazy world. Kurt had no idea what the hell had happened to her, and may never find out in full, so he needed to trace her movements back to her.

The truck stop was about another ten miles from a small town where the family who'd originally adopted the dog had lived, and then the brother was another six miles approximately past that—and he was the one now in jail, the one who apparently knew nothing about the dog. How convenient for everybody. Kurt just shook his head, thinking about what Sabine had probably been through all this time. Most of the world would probably just say, *Forget it, shoot the dog*, and move on.

Kurt wasn't built that way. Every one of the animals on this earth deserved a chance, particularly when it was a human who had messed them up in the first place. Still, Kurt could only do so much, and the first thing was to see if he could find that dog.

As he drove by familiar places, memories plagued him. He'd had a girlfriend off and on throughout high school, but, since he was headed down a dark and windy path back then, he knew he needed to break away from her. Her parents had been totally against their association, and, even though the teens had snuck around as much as they could, it had been hard to continue their relationship. Yet it had also added to the danger and the joy.

He shook his head as he turned onto the main freeway, heading toward the truck stop. It didn't make any sense to even have these memories at this point in time. He didn't know why Laurie Ann's voice popped into his head. It'd been thirteen years since he'd seen her. He had gone to her the night before he was due to leave, and she'd pushed him away. She had been indifferent, almost antagonistic, and he'd been heartbroken. But still he had hidden behind the tough skin that he'd been known for and had walked away from her.

Thinking about it now, he felt it was the best thing he could have done. For him. For her. Besides, he was a completely different person now. Kurt wondered if she was still around. She'd had a huge potential to become something. She'd planned to go into med school, but he didn't know whether that dream had panned out or not. She had the smarts. He could have had the smarts too, but that would have meant applying himself. She was a good girl, and he was a bad boy from across the tracks. They didn't stand a chance. They'd met often—at least as often as they could—but definitely a huge gap existed between them.

He liked to think of her as his foray into the good side of life that had made him go into the navy. And, although she didn't want him to go, she did not stand in his way. He appreciated that about her. But thirteen years later? Well, that was a long time. She probably had a half-dozen kids and could be anywhere at the moment.

He kept driving, now discovering the truck stop was farther away than he'd thought. He checked his GPS and noted it had been moved out of town when the city itself had enlarged. He certainly didn't remember the truck stop, but, as he finally came upon the location that he was looking for, it was twenty miles out of town. He'd passed by a couple smaller clutches of homes, and now he was pulling into a huge truck stop. It made a lot more sense to put it way out here, but, at the same time, this fact threw off his distance and timing calculations.

He pulled up, hopped out, and stretched his legs. That was the thing about injuries; the one thing he had to do on a constant basis was stretch. Otherwise his muscles would cramp, and stiffness would set in very quickly. The place was busy here, huge semis parked on the left and lots of other traffic. The truck stop had what appeared to be close to fifty individual gas pumps; it was a sight to behold. More and more of these bigger stations popped up all across the states. He walked slowly toward the restaurant, as he eyed the area. He stepped inside; the din from the patrons rose all around him. A waitress stepped up in front and asked if he wanted a table. He nodded slightly and said, "Yes, just for coffee though."

She nodded and brought him to a small booth by the window at the back. It was a perfect location. He smiled, thanked her, and sat down. He pulled the menu that she'd given him closer. He didn't really need food, considering he'd just eaten a couple sandwiches. But a piece of pie? Well, that would never go wrong. She brought him a mug of coffee almost immediately. He thanked her and ordered a piece of apple pie to go with it. She laughed and asked, "Ice cream or not?"

"Not today," he said with a smile, and the waitress disappeared.

Just then a woman in the booth ahead of him with her back to Kurt said, "What's apple pie without ice cream? Isn't that like a kiss without the squeeze?"

He froze and stared at the waves of auburn hair before him. "Laurie Ann?"

She turned in her booth and gave him a droll smile. "Well, you're not somebody I ever expected to see again."

He just stared. She still had the same heart-shaped face, huge blue eyes, long lashes, and that damn dimple in the corner of her cheek that set him off every time. He shook his head. The older Laurie Ann settled in front of him was still as beautiful but had matured into something completely different.

"I literally just arrived," he said, as he motioned at the booth seat across from him. "Join me?"

She hesitated, then shook her head. "No time. I'm late." She checked her watch, looked at him, smiled, and said, "Another time. Maybe thirteen more years?"

"Or in the next few days?" he asked.

She hesitated as she stood, and she was still the same tall slim beauty that he'd known before. "How long are you in town for?" she asked hesitantly.

"I'm looking for a missing K9 War Dog," he said.

Her eyebrows shot up. "Are you still in the navy?"

"No," he said.

"Well, must have been something major to take you away from that," she said. "Absolutely nothing would deter you back then."

"And yet you never asked me to stay." As soon as the words were out of his mouth, he wished he hadn't said anything, but the surprised look on her face told him that she had never thought that he'd noticed or cared.

"No," she said gently. "It was something very close to your heart, and I didn't want to ruin that."

He nodded slowly. "It was the making of me," he said. "It really straightened me up, and I became a very different man."

Her eyebrows lifted.

"I know," he said with a sideways grin. "A lot of room for growth."

She chuckled. "You were a good person," she said. "I don't know who you are now, but I'm happy for you if you're happier with you."

It was a little convoluted, but he understood.

Just then her phone rang, and she winced. "I've really got to go," and she turned and raced down the aisle.

His waitress came back, bringing his pie. He looked at her, smiled, and said, "An old friend I wasn't expecting to meet," he said, motioning at Laurie Ann.

"She comes in here a fair bit," she said. "She's a pediatrician and runs between several counties."

"Ah." He sat back with his pie, a big smile on his face. A pediatrician. He rolled that around in his mind and smiled. It was perfect; she had always been a fan of families and children.

"I'm glad for her," he murmured, but the waitress was long gone. And he sat here, almost dazed, wondering how something so simple as coming back home had opened up such interesting wounds. He was proud of who he was now; he was not proud of who he'd been back then. He hadn't really known any better, and that was no excuse. He was just so determined to get out and to prove himself and to be somebody whose early beginnings had fallen by the wayside. He was sure the shrinks would have a heyday with a lot of it.

In fact, some of the ones he'd talked to had helped; some of them hadn't. Even having somebody to talk it out with and to not judge him for all his early mistakes had been a good thing. But, even now, just seeing her again had been almost heartbreaking. He knew he'd missed a huge opportunity when he had walked away from her. They were so young then, and he even more than most. But he was really happy for her—a pediatrician. Wow.

He shook his head and dug into his pie.

LAURIE ANN SAT in the car, shaking for a good five minutes before she could get a grip on herself and headed out. Sure she was late, but that wasn't the real reason. It was seeing Kurt like that, out of the blue. Of course he hadn't told her that he was coming; he didn't even know how to get hold of her. He hadn't said anything because they hadn't kept in touch. But why would they? He was headed to the military to take over and to save the world, and she'd been heading to med school or at least pre-med at that point in time.

She had managed to make her dream happen, even if it had taken a few extra years to get there. But then her son, Jeremy, was never something that she ever regretted having, but how was she now supposed to tell his father about their son, especially when she hadn't told him back then? She hadn't made any attempt to tell him before he left. She had kept that secret, knowing that he would have likely stayed in town, hating his life and hating everything about it, when he had been so desperate to get away. For her to let him go was the best thing for him.

She had known that at the time, and she hadn't even told her parents. It had all been so damn new back then; she was only weeks pregnant when Kurt left, and it had been a tough adjustment. Her parents had not been very accepting, and that was to put it mildly. If it weren't for Sally, her older sister, Laurie Ann didn't know what she would have done.

Even now, her relationship with her parents was remotely cordial but not even close to warm. They weren't trying to make up for lost time with Jeremy, which hurt more than their rejection of her and more than the fact they had practically kicked her out of the house for refusing to terminate her pregnancy. She found it hard to forgive and to forget. Didn't say much about her, did it?

She sat there for a long moment, then finally turned on the engine and drove to work. She needed the job; she needed the work for her own sanity, if nothing else. She'd come a long way in these last few years, but just seeing Kurt like that again? It was as if she hadn't moved forward. As in not at all. And how sad was that?

Jeremy was everything to her. He'd been an easy baby and was a good kid. He wasn't aggressive or messed up, like his father had been at that age. Even now, she looked back and didn't know what the initial attraction had been. But, like a moth to a flame, she couldn't resist. No matter how much she tried to explain her relationship with Kurt to her parents, they just weren't having it. There was no understanding in their worldly eyes. She'd made a colossal mistake with the worst person possible, and that was it. She had to live and let live, and they didn't want anything to do with her. Or Jeremy.

She could feel the tears collecting in the corner of her eyes, as she thought about all those tumultuous years. One of the things that had kept her going was that she knew it wouldn't be forever and that life would improve. It was mostly because of Kurt that she understood that lesson. After losing his mother, he'd gone wild and had a really rough time adapting to the loss. He'd also gone through a horrific time in foster care.

Laurie Ann hadn't understood it at the time, but she sure did afterward. Nothing like realizing your parents—who you thought would be there and would be supportive when you fell and would give you a hand up—had turned their backs on you and made you feel so much less of a person.

And no way, even now, would she let them refer to her actions as a mistake because Jeremy was the result, and she loved Jeremy with a love she had never expected to experience—outside of the sexual intimacy that she had gloried in with Kurt.

She pulled into the medical clinic. This had been her second dream—to become a doctor—and she'd made it. She'd achieved two things in her world that she had desperately wanted. She'd wanted kids, and she'd wanted to be a doctor, so why then did she feel like everything in her life was a complete and utter failure? She shook her head, exited the car, and headed out to start her day. This was the lifeline that had kept her going before, and obviously it would be the lifeline that kept her going now too.

CHAPTER 2

Laurie Ann walked out of the office four hours later, having treated all the cases lined up for the day. Normally she would head to another clinic for the afternoon, but apparently it was closed due to a flood in the bathroom. She was grateful for the time off, as she was already feeling the effects of trying to keep her emotions locked down to get through the hours so far. She checked her watch, anxious to get home and to be with Jeremy.

She hopped into her vehicle, turned the key, and drove her car straight home. As she passed the truck stop, she wondered if Kurt was still there. Of course he wasn't. No need for him to sit there for that many hours. When she finally pulled into her driveway, Jeremy sat on the front steps, talking with a buddy. They had skateboards out, and thankfully they had their crash helmets, knee pads, and elbow pads on. As she walked toward them with a bright smile, Jeremy looked at her and asked, "How come you're home so early?"

She quickly explained about the flood at the second clinic. "How are you two guys doing?"

"Great," he said. "School has been out since lunch."

"I thought you had one class this afternoon," she said smoothly, knowing full well he did.

He nodded. "Yes, but the teacher called in sick, so the

class was called off. Since it's the only class I have this afternoon, I'm home."

"And you too, Frank?"

"Yeah, same class as Jeremy," he said in a careless tone.

She nodded and stepped past them. "Just don't break anything, huh?"

They both chuckled, got up, grabbed their skateboards, and headed down the sidewalk. The speeds they went sometimes scared her, but she was enough of a trusting mother to let them go do their thing. She already knew that to hold them back would be the opposite effect that she wanted.

As she walked inside, she headed for the coffeepot. She was drinking way too much caffeine these days, but it was pretty hard to do anything else. And after today, seeing Kurt, she knew that it would take coffee to keep her going. With the coffee dripping—thankfully just a small two-cup pot—she decided an awful lot of housecleaning needed to get done. It seemed a shame to take her afternoon off to clean house, but sometimes it was the better answer for keeping her mind occupied.

She got out her rubber gloves and her spray bottles and was working in the bathroom, when her sister called. "Well, as much as I love any interruption from cleaning bathrooms," she said to her sister, "you only call when you have a reason."

"Somebody saw Kurt in town," her sister said without any preamble.

"That's nice," Laurie Ann said calmly. "I saw him this morning."

A horrified gasp came from the other end of the phone. "What? Why didn't you tell me?"

"Nothing to tell," she said. "I stopped in for a bite to eat. After staying up all night, I didn't have time this morning to fix breakfast. So I stopped in at the truck stop and had coffee and one of their danishes."

"You know that you shouldn't be living on sugar," her sister said irritably. "You're a doctor. You should know better."

"I also know that sugar is what gives me energy, and I needed something to get through the morning," she snapped.

"What about Kurt? Did you call him?"

"I haven't seen or contacted Kurt since he left town thirteen years ago," she said for what had to be the thousandth time over the last decade plus. "He was sitting behind me. I saw him as he came down the aisle. I couldn't believe it, but then I recognized his voice."

"And did you get up and run out of there?"

"I don't run from anything these days," she snapped. "Now did you have a reason for calling? Otherwise I'm going back to cleaning the bathroom."

"Why aren't you at work?" her sister snapped back.

"Look. The second clinic had a flood in their bathroom, so everybody was sent home, and I'm just taking the opportunity to get some housekeeping done."

"Well, you only clean house when you're upset," her sister said, in that same shrewd tone that said she knew too much about Laurie Ann already.

"No," she said. "I just have a busy weekend planned, and I didn't want to ruin it, trying to get all this stuff done at the same time."

"Oh," Sally said. "Did you talk to him?"

"Yes, I did," she said.

"And?" Sally asked after a moment, when Laurie Ann didn't volunteer anything.

"And what?" she said. "We exchanged some basic greetings. *How are you? How's life been treating you?* That was it. I was late for work, got up, and left."

"Okay," Sally said, "but make sure you avoid him in the future."

"Just like I said already, I don't run anymore," she repeated. She sprayed the bathtub with the phone tucked into her shoulder and said, "If there's nothing else, let me get back to my cleaning."

"You're not seeing him again, right?"

"Stop worrying, Sally," she said. "We have to take every step forward in life that we can. I'll not allow his return to hold me back."

"I know that, but what if he finds out?"

"It's been on my mind a lot anyway," she said. "What if he does find out? What do you want me to do? Ignore him? I don't think so."

"You can't tell him," Sally said, horrified.

"I'll cross that bridge when I get there," she said wearily. "Now, if you don't mind, I'm going back to my cleaning." In frustration, she hung up, put the phone on the counter beside her, and then she attacked the bathtub ring with a vengeance. Ever since she'd gotten pregnant, her family had treated her as if she were an innocent gullible fool. And that, even now, she would go running back into Kurt's arms.

As she thought about it, she wondered if maybe she would. He was older and more mature, and something was clearly different about him from the bad boy she'd known. But still that same frisson of attraction existed between them. That had partly been the reason why she'd been so grateful for a chance to leave the coffee shop. It had been such a shock to see him. Yet he was on her mind most days because of Jeremy. Why the hell should her son not have a father? It's not as if she'd given Jeremy a choice, and she hadn't given his father a choice either. But it was just one more of those things in life that she had to sort out for herself, and she didn't quite know how to do that.

"Mom?" Jeremy called out.

"I'm upstairs in the bathroom, cleaning," she called out. He raced up the stairs. She groaned and said, "Are those dirty shoes you have on?"

"Yeah," he said, "but I'm leaving right away."

"Where are you going?" she asked.

"Can I go over to Frank's house?"

"Yes, but I want you home before five."

He groaned.

"Home before five, or you can't go," she said in that calm voice that she always used with him.

"Fine." And he bolted off.

She smiled because of all the things that she'd done well, raising Jeremy was one of them. He was a good kid, and it just made it all that much harder to wonder if he was missing out on that whole father-bonding thing because she hadn't bothered to tell Kurt that he would be a father.

KURT WALKED AROUND the truck stop for a couple hours, looking for any sign that the War Dog was around. He talked to the staff currently on duty, but the shift changed in another hour, and then he would speak to the new staff. He wandered all along the edge of the gravel area leading to the bushes, where they thought they'd seen the dog, but nothing fresh remained. He sat inside the shrubs for a good hour, waiting to see if anything would approach. So far nothing. He got up and walked a good one hundred yards into the treed area and circled around the truck stop another one hundred yards back of the pavement.

Animals were attracted to humans because of the food supply, and, in this case, maybe also because human companionship is what Sabine knew. But, if she'd had a few bad months, it would make her wary, and she wouldn't get too much closer to Kurt. After he did the one pass, he went out another one hundred yards farther into a bigger and wider pass. Again nothing, although he saw bits and pieces of golden fur on the bushes.

It was almost impossible to tell how fresh they were after the rain last night. He wasn't seeing any fresh tracks, but he knew that Sabine had to be somewhere around here. At least in the last couple days. As he slowly made his third and final wide path around, he stopped at a fallen tree and just sat here.

"Sabine," he called out softly. "Sabine, I'm here for you. Let me help you, little one."

Of course there was no answer.

After he rested a bit, he resumed walking slowly, calling out to her every once in a while in a gentle voice, letting her know that he was around. He returned to the fallen tree and put some treats on the stump for her. The birds might get them, but maybe she would too. And he kept walking around to the next point. He stopped listening to the trucks coming and going, even though they were there nearby, but it remained dim in the background of his primary focus.

He noted another tree stump up ahead. He put a few

treats on it, and he walked ten feet forward and then slowly stopped. He tilted his head but didn't turn around. He smiled at the gentle rustling in the bushes. "Are you stalking me, Sabine?"

He twisted ever-so-slightly and looked behind him but couldn't see her. But he had that inner sense that he was being watched. It could be something else, but he was hoping that the only thing out here looking and following him would be the dog he was after. He kept going, carefully keeping an eye on the world around him, but she never showed herself. Just before he walked back toward the pavement, he dropped one more pile of treats and then kept on going.

"I'll be back tomorrow," he said. "I've got to find a place to stay for the night and to see about getting the rest of my equipment. I'll return in the morning." And he headed toward his truck.

As he got there, a group of teens—five of them—hung around his rental.

"Can I help you?" he said.

One of the kids looked at him guiltily.

"You got a problem?" Kurt asked him.

The guy immediately started to bluster. "Hey, we thought it was stolen."

"Yeah, what would make you think it was stolen?" he asked. "It's got rental stickers all over it."

They just shrugged and said, "Hell, we didn't know that."

"Ah, because it says it right there." And he pointed it out.

"Hey, smart-ass," one of the kids said, "you don't have to be nasty."

"That's nasty?" he asked with his eyebrows tilted.

"Whatever," the first guy said. "Come on, guys. Let's leave it."

"Yeah, good idea," Kurt said. "Leave the truck alone."

"I've got nothing to do with you, old man."

At that, he snorted. "I'm an old man? What are you? Still in diapers?"

One of the guys turned and sneered at him. "You don't want to push it," he said. "We don't take kindly to strangers around here."

"Well, if you think I'm scared, think again," he said. "I'm not scared of little punks like you."

At that, the guy roared, turned around, and came at him, running. Kurt braced himself for the blow and just before the kid caught up to him, Kurt smacked him hard with a hook right into the elbow swinging his way. As soon as he connected with the bone, the kid started screaming.

"Oh, my God, oh, my God," he said, "you broke my arm."

"Wow, that's funny. How could I break your arm when you were the one attacking me?"

"Well, I saw everything," his friend said. "You attacked him."

Kurt laughed. "You think video cameras aren't all around the truck stop?"

At that, the boys turned and looked at the cameras. One of the guys said, "Come on, Quinsy. Let's go."

"Fuck off," Quinsy said. "He fucking broke my arm."

"Come on. We have to get out of here," the other kid snapped.

"My arm is broken! Remember?"

"Let's go get it looked at." Finally, at the other one's insistence, the kids took off.

The last thing Kurt wanted was any more trouble. But, when trouble came his way, he didn't back down.

And then a voice behind him said, "I didn't think I'd see that day."

He stopped, frowned, and turned to look at a cop standing nearby, his hands on his hips, studying Kurt carefully. He looked at him, and then the memory hit. "Well, well, well, if it isn't Amos Packard," he said.

"*Detective* Amos Packard, if you don't mind," he said, crossing his arms. "It really is you, isn't it?"

"Well, it's certainly me," Kurt said. "Funny how, in my first day back in town, I see two people I know. Who'd have thought it?"

"Well, I can say that I fully expected you to be in trouble again."

He looked at him in surprise, then looked at the kids. "That wasn't trouble," he said. "They were just kids in trouble."

"You would recognize that, wouldn't you?"

He nodded slowly. "Yeah, I sure would. I was a pain in the ass back then, wasn't I?"

"Yep, you sure were," Amos said. "The question is, are you still?"

He grinned at him. "Thirteen years in the navy, as a Navy SEAL, before I was medically discharged." He watched the shock and the surprise in Amos's eyes.

"Seriously?"

Kurt nodded. "The US Navy was the best thing for me," he said. "It took a bit, and I didn't learn quickly, but I did eventually learn and straightened up pretty decent too."

"Wow," he said; then he frowned. "Medically discharged?"

"Yes, an underwater accident," he said. "Took my lower leg, compromised my lungs, crushed a few ribs." He shrugged and said, "You know how accidents happen."

"Apparently," he said. Studying Kurt's legs, he asked, "You lost a leg?"

For that answer, Kurt reached down and hitched up his jeans, so Amos could see the prosthetic.

"Wow, okay then. So what are you doing back in town?"

"I'm here," Kurt said, wondering if maybe Amos would be of help, "looking for a War Dog last seen in this vicinity."

Amos frowned. "War Dog?" he asked cautiously.

Kurt explained the problem.

"Interesting," Amos said. "I did hear a dog was around here and that she was attacking people."

"Well, I don't know that Sabine would attack people," Kurt said, "because that certainly wouldn't be normal behavior for her."

"Normal or not," he said, "that's the rumors and that's the reports we've had."

"Anybody find her yet?"

The detective shook his head. "No, not yet. So you are looking for it too?"

"I am. I thought maybe she was following me in the bush back here. But I didn't catch sight of her."

"Well, I certainly won't be upset if you catch her," the detective said, "because that's an open case, and we're still trying to find her before she attacks somebody else."

"Well, I guess it depends on who she was attacking. If it was stupid kids like that, who were just looking for trouble, then they deserve every bite they get," he said calmly, leaning against the rental truck, his arms over his chest, as he studied the detective. He understood that there would be a certain amount of bad feelings between him and the community because he had certainly caused his own share of trouble. "And I'm not here to cause trouble for anybody. I want to save the dog."

"Interesting," Amos murmured, as he studied Kurt. "I really want to believe that you've had a change of heart and have done some growing up, but I'm not sure anybody will put the time and effort into a dog like that."

"And isn't that just too damn bad that that's hard to believe?" Kurt said. "But if you don't trust me, you can call my boss." And he gave him Badger's card, with the number for Titanium Corp.

"Fine," he said, "I will do that."

"Good. In the meantime, I have to find a motel or a place to stay."

"And please stay out of trouble," the detective said, shooting him a hard glance, as he walked back to his cruiser.

"Always," Kurt murmured. He hopped into his truck and turned on the engine and waited, windows open for the heat, until the detective left. Then he pulled the truck slowly forward, and, just as he pulled out, a shot rang out, and a force slammed into his shoulder.

He hit the brakes and fell over sideways out of sight, as he lay here, swearing to himself.

His shoulder burned hard and fast and he didn't know if the bullet had gone in or if it was just a burn. He clamped his hand tight around the injury, as he searched the front of the truck for something to stop the bleeding. That shot had been targeted just a little too perfectly *after* the detective was gone for it to be accidental.

In his mind Kurt could see the five kids first and foremost as the shooters. But he couldn't prove that. Not without the cameras. He lay still, listening for footsteps coming closer, but instead heard several running away, not coming to help. Or to hurt. He shifted so he could look in the direction of whoever was taking off. He fired up the truck and, holding his shoulder, drove after them.

The five kids were up ahead, one holding a handgun. They took one look at Kurt and screamed in terror. He drove the truck right inside the group, splitting them up. Another vehicle raced around him, and the kids bailed into the new vehicle. Kurt, swearing at the interference, tried to read the license plate as they took off. It appeared to be smeared with mud and was illegible.

He didn't know if the detective was still around or if he'd even give a shit. But, in this case, Kurt was an innocent citizen, and that wouldn't wash in his world. He pulled off to the far corner of the parking lot and swore now at the pain in his shoulder. He didn't want to go to a hospital ever again, and he sure as hell didn't want to deal with doctors' questions or cops called because of a gunshot wound. Kurt had to figure out what he would do with those damn kids, but first and foremost he needed his shoulder looked at. He thought about his options for a long time.

"It's a bad idea. Don't do it," he muttered. "But then, if not that, what?"

He pulled out his phone and looked her up online. She still had the same name. She lived about twenty minutes from here. He hadn't found an online mention of her cell phone number yet, but, when he saw her name at a clinic and a cell phone for after-hours assistance, he quickly dialed it.

When he heard her voice on the other end, he said, "I

don't have any right to ask you"—without bothering to identify himself—"but I need an injury looked after."

"Kurt?" she asked. "What's the matter?"

"I'm back at the truck stop, looking for the dog," he said. "I've been here all afternoon, and five kids came out of nowhere, and one shot me."

"Oh, my God," she cried out. "Go to the hospital."

"No, I don't want to do that. Do you remember Amos Packard, the local cop? He already warned me to stay out of trouble."

"That's very presumptuous of him," she said flatly. "He doesn't know anything about you."

"No, and neither do you by rights," he said. "But I was really hoping you could check to make sure the bullet was out."

"You know that I'm a pediatrician, right? I'm not a *doctor* doctor."

"Oh, that's *doctor* doctor enough for me, as far as I'm concerned."

"You really need to go to the hospital," she said calmly.

"And that'll just bring up all kinds of questions which I don't want to deal with."

"You do have a legitimate reason for being here, don't you?"

"Yes," he said. "I told you about it."

"Well then, go to the hospital," she said, "and get it looked after."

He swore and said, "Fine," and tossed his phone on the bench seat, but he didn't hang up the call. He reached for the glove box to see if anything inside there could be useful.

"What are you doing?" she asked through the phone suspiciously.

"I'll look after the damn thing myself," he said.

"Don't do that," she said. "It'll get infected."

"Well, I won't start opening up case files and bothering the cops. You know they'll take one look at me, remember my history, and then just say something like *You deserve it.*"

"Well, I would hope not." But doubt was in her tone.

"You know that's what they'll do," he said. "You'd like to think that they won't give a shit about the past, but Amos already warned me. Besides, this isn't bad," he said. "I just need some antiseptic to clean it up. I'll go to the drugstore and get it."

"Don't bother," she said. "Come here."

At the resignation in her tone, he snorted. "Don't do me any favors. I don't owe you anything, and you don't owe me anything," he said. "I'll just go to a drugstore."

"Covered in blood?" she asked calmly. "I've got everything I need here." She quickly ran off her address and said, "I expect you in twenty."

He snorted at that, but he headed down the highway in her direction. He just hoped, with the pain kicking in, that the damage wasn't more than he thought. It didn't seem like it was more than a flesh wound, but it was killing him regardless, and that worried him a bit. As he pulled into her driveway, he watched a couple kids skateboarding up and down the road. That was something he'd never had a chance to do. Not the activity itself. Not the time spent with like-minded people either.

At that stage in his life, Kurt had been still fighting for food on the streets.

The front door to the house opened, and there she stood in shorts and a T-shirt, hands on her hips, as she glared at him.

He shut off the engine, opened up the truck door, and hopped out, almost dropping to his knees. He grabbed the truck door to hold himself upright, and she was there in a heartbeat. He wrapped his arm around her, and she said, "I didn't think I came home early today for this, but now I have to wonder."

And he closed his eyes and said, "I didn't think I needed help either."

"You needed help back then too," she said, "but you wouldn't let me get close enough."

He smiled at the memories, as she half supported him inside the house and then into the kitchen. When he finally sat down on a kitchen chair, he said, "If I go to sleep, just let me sleep. Okay?"

"Nope," she said. "You pass out on me, then I am calling an ambulance."

"You always were a hard-ass," he murmured.

"Yep, sure was," she said.

"I always loved that," he said.

She snorted. "You couldn't have proven it by me."

"Yeah, I feel like I should have stayed in town, but I knew it was bad news for me," he murmured. "And, even worse, it was bad news for you."

"I'm not sure what brought this on," she said, "but it was a long time ago. Time to move on with your life."

Not a whole lot he could say about that. It was the truth.

CHAPTER 3

Laurie Ann quickly pulled his T-shirt up over his shoulder and whistled. "That's an ugly burn."

"But it's just a burn, right?"

"Well, it went through the top of the upper arm and shoulder. That's an odd trajectory."

"I had just lifted my arm to move the sun visor."

"And so you shifted away from where you were sitting straight?"

"Yeah," he murmured. "And I figured that's what saved my life."

"They were gunning for you?" She stared at him in horror.

"It was the kids," he said. And he explained, slowly, enunciating carefully, as she listened to the pain in his voice.

"Wow," she murmured. "You're still a hard-ass too, aren't you?"

"Would I let the five of them beat me up? No," he murmured. "You know that'll never be anything I can do."

"No, and you shouldn't have to," she said. "I'm surprised you didn't lay all five of them on the ground."

"Maybe, if I knew just where they were at, I would have," he said, describing how the unmarked vehicle took the gang of kids away. He took a long slow deep breath. She held out the alcohol to clean his wound, and he nodded. As soon as the antiseptic solution washed over the open wound, he sucked in his breath and closed his eyes, willing himself not to screech like a two-year-old.

"It's almost done," she said. "Any idea where the bullet is?"

"It's probably in the damn back seat of the truck," he said. "It didn't get that far."

"You'll have to wash out the truck too. A lot of blood is on your shirt, so I'm sure some is on the truck seat."

"I know," he said, "but the inside of the vehicle isn't exactly what I'm worrying about at the moment."

"No, let's get this taken care of." She looked at it for a long moment and then shook her head. "You need some stitches in this."

"So put them in," he said.

"I can't just turn around and do that. You should go to a clinic," she said in exasperation.

He looked at the wound in surprise. "Then bring me the supplies, and I'll stitch it."

She stared at him in shock, wondering if he was serious, but the look on his face said not only was he serious but that he'd done it before.

"Knothead," she muttered.

"Yep, still the same knothead you used to know and love."

"True. That was a long time ago."

"It was a good thing I left."

She nodded. "It was, indeed."

"I straightened up and became somebody," he said quietly. "I would have ended up dead—probably murdered in some back alley—if I'd stayed."

"Oh, I don't doubt it," she said. "Believe me. I'm not

arguing with you."

He snorted. "Of course not, but I'm not a bad person."

"You weren't a bad person back then either," she said quietly. "I'll be back in a minute." She returned with a medical kit.

He studied her with interest. "Your family hated me."

She just gave him half a smile. "Yeah, they did, but," she added, "nothing was wrong with you back then. You just needed a way to straighten up and to find some purpose in life."

"The navy gave that to me," he murmured. "Best thing I ever did."

"I'm glad to hear that. I really am," she murmured.

He looked up at her, smiled, and said, "As much as I wanted to stay with you, I was more afraid of dragging you into the gutter where I was."

She looked at him, smiled, and said, "I really do understand."

"And I'm glad," he said, "because, at the time, I didn't even understand—not until later—when I realized just how much I'd improved my life and what I was like before."

"I hear you," she said. "I didn't ask you to stay because I also knew that you needed to go."

"The things that we do when we're young and stupid, huh?"

"Exactly," she said with a chuckle, "but it's not all bad."

"I know. Not all bad," he said. He looked at her searchingly. "So did you marry and have kids?"

"Something like that," she said lightly.

"Divorced?"

"Never bothered with the marrying."

"Wow," he said. "I thought for sure you would have

married and had your four kids, a fancy little house in suburbia with a white picket fence." As he looked around, he nodded. "This is kind of what I always thought of you having."

"Maybe," she said, "although I would love a place a little farther out of town."

"We all would," he said. "All the time I was recovering from the accident, all I could think about was my life being in the navy. But I can't do that anymore now, so what would I do?"

"And did you find answers for that? What will you do? Unless tracking down dogs is one of them?"

Such curiosity and honesty were in her question, so he answered in the same way. "I'm doing it as a favor for Titanium Corp. They were the ones who helped me get rehabilitated into work life again," he said. "When they told me the dog was missing in this area, I jumped at it."

"Of course. You've always loved animals."

"Well, my father raised them," he said. "At least before he tossed me into the foster system."

"I don't think he tossed you in it as much as he was a drunk, and you got pulled away from him."

"At thirteen, it made me a very angry young man."

"That it did," she said. She finished the stitching and put some antiseptic gel and a bandage on his shoulder. "There you are. All stitched back up again."

He looked down at it, nodded, and said, "Thanks. Those are handy skills."

"Sounds to me like you've already doctored yourself a few times."

"I had to," he said. "Sometimes, on missions, you don't get a whole lot of choices."

She nodded. "And I'm glad to hear that because it shows a complete change from who you were to who you are now."

"You have no idea," he said with a big grin. "As much as I don't like who I was, I certainly understand that that person is who I needed to be in order to understand where I am now."

"Good," she said with a gentle smile. "And stop being so hard on the person you were. I really loved that man." He gave her a warm smile that made her heart pound.

"I'm glad to hear that," he said, "because he really needed to be loved. Because he didn't love himself."

"Absolutely," she said. "Well, this seems oddly familiar." She motioned at him, sitting here at the kitchen table. "Remember?"

One of the times when Kurt had been badly beaten up, he came running to her, and she'd fixed his nose and some of the bruises and cuts on his arms. "You were always telling me back then how you would be a doctor," he murmured.

"Well, I did get caught that night by my parents," she said. "I was grounded for weeks afterward."

"Right. I came to your bedroom." He shook his head. "If I should ever have a daughter, I'll be horrified at the thought of all those men out there, ready to prey on her."

"Yet you weren't preying on me," she said. "You were coming home."

He looked at her in surprise and then nodded slowly. "I was," he said, "and that makes it all the sadder."

"Yes, and no," she said. "It also is very enlightening."

"Maybe. Did you have a good thirteen years?" he asked, his gaze still searching, still curious as he pulled his t-shirt on.

She turned away and busied herself, cleaning up. She didn't know what to say.

"Or not, I gather?"

"Well, I had some absolutely incredible moments," she said, thinking about the birth of her son. "And then some really tough moments. School was difficult. I did get through med school though. As you're well aware, I'm a pediatrician, and I had a child, so I have those two things I really wanted out of my life."

"Absolutely. So where's your child? Is it a boy or a girl?"

She turned, smiled, took a deep breath, and said, "A boy. His name is Jeremy."

"That's a good solid name," he said. "How old is he?"

Just then Jeremy and Frank dashed through the front door. "Hey, Mom. Who's here?"

As her hand came up, the two lanky teens came to a stop in the kitchen. Kurt looked on, as she didn't even know what to say to him. And then proper manners took over. "Jeremy, this is a friend of mine, Kurt. This is Jeremy, my son, and his friend, Frank."

Kurt looked at them both, pulling his shirt over the bandage, and smiled at the boys. "Hey, nice to meet you guys. Your mom and I are old friends. I left after graduation."

"Yeah, I don't remember meeting you before," Jeremy said, his focus completely on Kurt.

She looked at her son, wondering what was going through his mind. "We were in school together."

He looked at her and frowned and said, "Really?"

"Yes," she said. "He's in town looking for a missing War Dog."

"Oh, wow," Frank said. "What does that mean?"

And then Kurt explained the reason he was in town.

"I heard about that dog," Jeremy said. "I think it attacked some of those kids in the gang," he said, turning to Frank.

"Yeah, well, they're not much of a gang. They're just bullies."

"Five of them?" Kurt asked. The two boys looked at him in surprise. "I think I met them."

"Yeah, there's five of them."

"Or is there a sixth?" Kurt asked. "They rode off in a vehicle, but someone else was driving."

The two teens shrugged. Jeremy added, "An older guy hangs around with them a lot. Maybe they do stuff for him. I'm not sure." Jeremy lifted his eyebrows. "Did you see them?"

"Yeah, I met them at the truck stop," he said, with a sideways look at Laurie Ann.

She shook her head slightly, a plea in her gaze, hoping that Kurt wouldn't say anything more about who shot him.

"Yeah, they tend to hang around there a lot." Jeremy walked over to the sink and grabbed a glass of water.

"So the dog might have had a good reason for attacking them, huh?"

"Are you kidding? Absolutely would have a reason. Nothing good about those kids."

"That's too bad," Kurt said. "I've heard that a time or two about other young men."

"Some of them are salvageable," Jeremy said, "but not these ones."

She stepped in at that point. "What are you two guys up to?"

"We want to get soda pop," he said, "please."

She groaned, reached for her purse, and handed over a twenty-dollar bill. "Bring me back the change."

They grabbed the twenty and raced out. She shook her head. "He just gets so big every day."

"He is big," Kurt said, eyeing her intently.

"I know. It's a bit of a shock all the time," she said with a smile.

"He also looks familiar," Kurt said in an odd voice.

She looked at him, hesitant. "In what way?"

"Well, he's definitely got your hair and your eyes," he said, his voice hardening. "But then he's also got my nose, my jaw, and my size," he said in a frigid voice. "Were you ever going to tell me?"

She just stared at him, too shocked to even answer it.

He stood, the chair screeching, almost falling over, and turned toward her. "Were you going to tell me that I had a son?"

She shook her head mutely. She hadn't expected him to recognize his son so fast, so soon. And how would she answer him now?

"No?" he asked in outrage.

She held up her hand. "Yes, I planned to tell you," she said, "but, after you left, I didn't know how to. As soon as I realized that you were here in town, I thought it was a perfect opportunity—one I've been thinking about for a couple years."

"You've been *thinking*. For *two years*," he said, "but did you know that you were pregnant before I left?"

She took a slow deep breath, knowing that whatever chance at friendship they might have had was about to die right now, and she nodded. "Yes, but you were leaving in two weeks. What did you want me to do? Tell you that I was carrying your child and have you tell me to get an abortion? Or have you stay behind, that same angry young man who hated his life here and who would hate me for chaining him to this life? I let you go, and I had Jeremy," she said, "and it was the best decision of my life."

He stared at her, as if not knowing what to say.

"And, if you think it was an easy yes-or-no decision, you're right. It was. However, it wasn't an easy choice to then deal with the day-to-day living," she said. "Although I would have done anything to have Jeremy, yet raising him on my own, without my parents, was not easy."

KURT STARED AT her in shock, and, at the same time, a part of him wanted to throw his arms around her and hold her close. He exhaled a long breath and took a step back.

Laurie Ann winced at that movement more than anything. "I didn't know what to do," she said, "but I refused to give up my child."

He shook his head, not knowing what to say.

"There's no way," she said, "that you wouldn't have hated your life, if forced to stay here, when you were so eager to go."

"I was a mess back then," he said, sitting down on the chair hard. All he could see was the tall, strapping young man who had been in the kitchen just moments before, knowing instinctively that he was his. "My God," he said as he looked at her. "I don't mean to besmirch your honor or anything else, but is there any doubt?"

"No," she said, "none."

He sagged into the chair and sat, frozen. He knew she was worried about him. Hell, he was worried about him too. Of all the blows he'd taken in life, this one had knocked his feet out from under him. He didn't even know how to feel. He was relieved that she'd decided to carry his child, saddened that he had missed out on the child's life, horrified that he hadn't been here in the first place and that she hadn't even told him because she was trying to save him. Was he so pathetic and had he been such a mess that he didn't see anything else around him?

"You wouldn't have known," she said, as if reading his mind. "I didn't show for several months."

"Your parents?"

"They basically kicked me out of the house."

He blanched at that. "I never did like them."

"They never did like you," she said cheerfully.

He let his breath out with a *whoosh*. "And they had good reason. I knocked up their daughter and walked out."

She stopped, looked at him with a hard gaze, and said, "I know you were a mess back then, but you aren't now."

"No, I'm not now," he said, "but I missed something major in my life."

"We all miss things in life," she said. "I think the greatest gift we can give ourselves is to capture what we can and to hang on to what we hold in our hands. The rest is too intangible, and it's gone within seconds."

"I missed his entire life," he said, staring at her in shock. "You got to hold him. You got to watch his first step. You got to get up in the middle of the night and soothe him and make him feel better."

"Yes, I did," she said, "and that's why I couldn't terminate the pregnancy. And believe me. I was under an awful lot of pressure to do so."

He nodded. "I can imagine. Your parents were also fairly religious, and I didn't fit their mold of a good future son-in-law."

"Not only didn't fit the mold," she said, "you weren't here."

He winced. "And that all goes back to the fact that I would have stayed if I'd known."

"And where would that have taken us?" she asked quietly.

He looked at her with a pain-filled gaze. "You could have told me before now. I didn't have to lose all his life."

"Maybe," she said. "Maybe that's true. But, at the same time, when was I supposed to contact you? A year later? When he was one year old? Or on his fifth birthday, when you were probably off, for all I know, married with a whole life completely independent of me, of this place? You didn't ever want to come back here. Remember?"

"Nothing was here for me," he said sadly.

"And you say that," she said, "but I was always here."

"But I didn't know that," he said, looking at her in surprise. "All you talked about was leaving."

She tilted her head and studied him and then nodded. "I forgot that," she said. "I always did talk about leaving, didn't I?"

He nodded. "It's one of the reasons I think we spent as much time with each other before we left because we were both caught up in this need to get away. But I did, and you never did."

"No, I never did," she said calmly, "because I found home here instead."

"Where did you go after your parents?"

"My sister's."

He nodded slowly. "I remember she lived on her own, didn't she?"

"Yes, and she took me in and helped me raise Jeremy for the first few years while he was a baby. When I got accepted into med school, I pushed the start off for one year, but then I had to make a decision, if I would finally go or stay home with my child."

"How did you manage financially?"

"My grandmother. She passed away not long after Jeremy turned one, and she left me enough money to at least get started," she said. "I'm still paying off student loans. I applied for a lot of grants, and I did get some, but, as you can imagine, it was hard with a baby at home, trying to keep a roof over my head. If not for my sister, I never would have made it."

"I can't believe that you made it even now," he said. "I'm really proud of you."

She stared at him in shock.

"I know it's not what you expected to hear," he said, "and I'm still reeling with the pain of having lost all those years with Jeremy. I don't know how to reconcile that because I know I was an ass back then, and I know I needed to leave, and I also know that leaving was the best thing for me. But it wasn't the best thing for you, and that's very hard for me to accept."

She walked over, pulled out a chair, and sat down beside him, picking up his hand. "I wish you'd come back to town years ago. I finished school and only in the last year or two did it really occurred to me that maybe I wasn't being fair to Jeremy. I didn't know how to get a hold of you, but I didn't try either. So I've been feeling guilty as hell, and that made it very difficult."

"No, you wouldn't have known how to contact me," he said, staring off in the distance. "I had no ties here. I had nobody here to keep in touch with—except for you—and I knew that you were better off without me. All I could see was our life together here and me dragging you down to the level I was in, and that was not what I wanted for you. I wanted you to go to med school, to become a doctor, to become somebody, and to have that family you always wanted."

She gave him a misty smile. "And you gave me that," she said. "You just didn't know it."

"Until today." He pulled away his hand, looked at her, and shook his head. "It's a lot to take in."

"Yes," she said, "but you have no idea how happy I am that we're talking about it right now."

He searched her gaze, looking for a hint of deceit, but couldn't see any. "You were always one of the most honest people I ever knew," he said. "So this isn't about you being dishonest. Yet it does feel like a betrayal. But I don't know if it's a betrayal of you to me or of me to me," he murmured.

She reached out her hand again, grabbing his. "And I get the first one," she said, "because I feel betrayal too, but I feel like I betrayed my son by not giving him a father. And it did cross my mind, at one point in time, that maybe, just maybe, I should do something about giving him a father. But, every time I thought about it, it felt wrong."

He looked at her, dazed. "You mean, like, marry somebody else?"

"Yes," she said honestly. "Not the best idea if I didn't feel the emotions to go with it, but a lot of women have married for a lot less reasons," she admitted. "Security, companionship, help raising a child are all part and parcel of that."

He stared down at her hand that held his, and he laced

their fingers together. "When you're young and stupid, you don't really realize the consequences. I can't imagine how shocked and scared you were at the time."

"No," she said, "but you have to balance that with how absolutely delighted I was too."

His lips tilted. "You always wanted a child."

"I always wanted to be a mother, yes. I'd hoped to have more than one, but life being what it is ..." She shrugged. "I could probably afford the time off now, but, up until now, all I've done is raise Jeremy, go to school, and get established in my practice."

"But you've done it all," he said, allowing his amazement to show through. "I mean, I can't name more than a half-dozen people I've met in my entire life who could have done what you've done. Even then I don't know if they could have because they're all men," he said. "It's astronomical what you've been through, and you're still sane," he said with a laugh.

She grinned. "Well, I don't know about the sane part, but I'm working on it."

"Being a single parent is never easy."

"No, but he's a good kid," she said honestly with pride. "He's got a good head on his shoulders. He's not stupid about life. He knows that I had him out of wedlock and that his father took off to join the navy and that I didn't tell you."

"So you were honest all the time," he said, shaking his head. "I don't know, if our positions were reversed, if I could have been quite so honest back then."

"Remember how we used to sit out on the back porch, away from everybody, just spending time together, trying to decide exactly what it was that we wanted out of life? You were pretty damn honest about it back then."

"And yet here I wasn't thinking of leaving you behind with a child," he said. "My life wasn't easy, but I certainly wasn't trying to raise a kid on my own."

"If my grandmother and my sister hadn't been around, it would have been a lot harder. When my grandmother passed away, it was very difficult for me because she was one of my biggest supporters."

"She was a great woman," he said affectionately. "She used to give me hell all the time."

"Yeah, she was trying to protect me, I think," she said with a laugh. "She told me privately that she always thought you were the one."

"Well, I was the one all right. The one who got you pregnant." Even hearing the words made him shake his head.

"Now that we've had that out," she said, standing up, "I'll put on some coffee, and then you can tell me what happened this afternoon and what you'll do now."

"I don't know what I'll do now," he said.

"I meant about the dog," she said for clarity's sake.

"Ah," he said, wondering at how different his world looked now. He wanted to get to know his son. That meant staying close, and, for the first time, that didn't feel wrong. It felt right. Right now he very much felt like he didn't ever want to walk out that door again.

"I'm not sure yet," he said slowly. "I've got to find a place to stay for a couple days. I headed to a motel first, but then I stopped in at the truck stop to see what the lay of the land was, and I didn't get any farther."

"Well, I'm sure you can find a motel around here not too far from the truck stop," she said.

"That's the plan," he said, rubbing his face. He stood, looked at his shoulder, and said, "Thank you for this."

"Not a problem," she said. "Like I said, old times."

With that came a flash of heat, as he remembered a lot of the *other* old times. He nodded and took a step back, carefully distancing himself from the feelings overwhelming him. Not only had he missed seeing his child being born and being there for all the milestones, he'd also missed seeing the only woman he'd ever cared about carrying his child, and a sense of possessiveness rippled through him that he never would have thought was even possible. He took a long slow breath. "I need to leave."

"It's probably a good idea," she said, her voice catching in the back of her throat.

He nodded and turned suddenly, heading for the front door.

"Feel free to stop by again."

At the front door, he stopped and rested his head against the door. "Does he know?"

"That it's you? No," she said. He nodded, opened the door, and she asked, "Do you want him to?"

And his heart stopped; he turned to look at her and whispered, "If he would like to, yes," he said. "I feel like I already missed everything that was important in his life—and mine. I don't want to miss anything more."

"I hear you," she said, "but I think, at this stage and at his age, that'll be Jeremy's choice."

Kurt winced, nodded, and said, "Here's my card. You can always call me if he decides he wants something to do with his father." He handed her the card, feeling strangely formal, and then out of sorts. He gave her one last long glance and said, "I'm so sorry," and then he turned and left.

CHAPTER 4

As days went, this one had been a whopper. Laurie Ann was exhausted inside and out. She had put on coffee and then hadn't even offered Kurt any. Now she sat here, his card in her hand, wondering what she was supposed to do. When Jeremy returned home alone, not very long afterward, he walked into the door, loud, noisy, heading straight to the fridge. She shook her head and said, "Dinner soon. Don't ruin your appetite."

"Won't," Jeremy said, as he shoved his head into the fridge and came out with pepperoni sticks.

She groaned. "How can you eat so much?" she muttered.

"It's easy," he said. "I'm a growing boy." He turned and looked around and said, "He left, huh?"

"Yes, he did."

"I like him," Jeremy added. "Too bad he left."

"And why is that?"

"I don't know."

And, with that, he headed to his room, completely unconcerned, and she wondered how a child could just let things go. Adults hang on to issues for a long time, toss them around in their brains, until they looked at everything from every angle and still came up with nothing. Her son seemed to be remarkably free of all that mental turmoil that she saw with so many teenagers. She didn't know how he managed it, but somehow he seemed to just walk through life, light and easy. Her son returned to the kitchen, reaching for more pepperoni sticks, and asked, "How long is he staying?"

"Who?" she asked, shaking her head and looking up at him.

"Your friend."

"I'm not sure. He really is looking for the War Dog," she said. "After that, I don't know."

"That's so cool," he said, "just to think about what training that dog has had."

She looked up at him, noting the admiration in his voice. "That's true," she said. "The dog has been through a lot. Do you know anything about the dog?"

"Nah," he said. "Wish I did though."

"Well, thanks for not making up something so you sound like you know more than you really do," she said in a dry tone.

He laughed. "Yeah, that's not my deal. That's other guys' deal."

"So what is your deal?"

He shrugged. "I just get along with everybody."

"Why is that?" she asked, realizing something important was here.

"I don't know," he said. "I just figure, if I get along with everybody, then I won't have to worry about not getting along with anybody."

She frowned at that. "Meaning?"

"Meaning nothing," he said. "When's dinner?"

She groaned. "Every time we get to a meaningful conversation, I feel like you avoid it."

"It's only meaningful to you," he said with the same flippancy that she'd come to recognize whenever he got close to an issue.

"Does it bother you that you don't have a father?"

"Only sometimes," he said. "It'd be kind of cool if I did, but I don't know what I would do with one after all this time. I mean, it's not like he's come looking for me."

"I told you that he didn't know about you," she said, "so don't go changing that story."

"I know, but still, if you have a relationship with a girl, you come back and check on her, don't you?"

"No," she said in surprise, "most of the time not. You move on. You have another relationship, and old relationships just seem to fade away."

"Is that what happened when you met this guy from today?"

She looked at him, shocked. "What do you mean?"

"Well, it's obvious you two were close, and I've never met him before, so I don't know where he came from or what type of relationship you had."

"He was a really good friend in school," she said.

He nodded and stared at her with that odd look in his eyes. "What are you saying? Is he my dad?"

And her chest collapsed. This was so a day of unwelcomed and unintentional emotional overload.

When she didn't answer, he continued, "It's just ... you haven't had a relationship really, that I know of, since I was born—at least not in the last many years. You don't date," he said with a wave of his hand. "And you're really attractive and all that, so there's really no reason why. And, if this guy was a friend in high school, and you had me just after high school, and I saw the way the two of you looked at each other ..."

"I see," she said in a faint voice.

"And then there's the look of him."

"Meaning?" She tore her gaze away from her hands to face her son.

"I look like him," he said bluntly.

"Yes, you do," she said, taking a deep breath, "and, yes, he's your father."

He stared at her, and something she didn't know—but maybe anger—was in that gaze. He no longer looked like a young teenager. Something very painful and very adult was in that gaze.

"He just found out about you too," she said quietly.

"Right now? Today?"

She nodded. "Yes, right now, today."

"Wow. Damn, that's heavy."

She stared at him, hating the language, but realizing it wasn't the time to bring that up. "I think he feels that is pretty heavy right now too. He's alternating between angry, betrayed, and overjoyed."

"Angry at what?" Jeremy asked belligerently. "That I'm a boy, not a girl?"

"Angry at himself that he didn't check up on me. Betrayed by me that I didn't tell him and betrayed by the world maybe in some ways too because this is how life panned out. It's not what he intended. It's not what I intended either," she said quietly, feeling part of her shrink inside. This conversation was not how she intended it to go. It wasn't in any way, shape, or form the way she wanted it to be. Anger emanated from her son, and she wasn't sure who it was directed at. "Because he didn't know anything about you, it's been a bit of a shock."

"But he left today, didn't he?" And he turned and flung open the fridge with a snap.

"Yes, he left," she said. "He was also shot at today."

At that, Jeremy spun so fast to focus on her. "What?"

"Those five guys, who you know, attacked Kurt at the gas station. He beat one up earlier, and then they came back with a gun and shot him as he was driving."

"Well, how bad is he hurt?" he asked, as if his thoughts were suddenly realigning.

"Not too bad. He wouldn't go to the hospital. So I stitched him up here before you got home," she said, staring down at her hands. "He didn't want to go to the cops."

"Why?" he asked, suspicion immediately flaring in his voice.

She smiled, looked up at him. "Because he has a very rough history here with the local police, and they already have a long file on him. He was a troubled teen after his mother died, and he was taken away from his drunk father when Kurt was young. About your age actually. He was the epitome of a bad boy and always in trouble," she said. "He hated authority, and the cops hated him because he was forever getting into trouble."

"So maybe that explains why no police, but why no hospital?"

"I understand why he did that too," she said. "He was badly injured in the navy and spent months, almost a year, in a military hospital. He'd do just about anything to avoid them. So I stitched him up. It wasn't bad."

"But still …"

She could sense the doubt and the judgment in her son's voice. "You don't understand what he's been through either," she said.

"Is he still a badass?"

"Yes, but in a good way. He is, was," she corrected herself, "a Navy SEAL."

His eyes lit up, and she could see hero worship about to start.

"He joined the navy from high school. That was always his plan. So, when I found out I was pregnant, I didn't tell him because he was leaving in two weeks," she said. "I knew that his life here was so bad and that he needed to get out of town to straighten up."

"Did he?"

She watched as Jeremy's fingers slowly clenched and unclenched on the counter behind him, and she nodded. "He did, and he did a beautiful job of it," she said with a smile. "He always was a good person, even in his teens, but now everybody can see that he's a good man too."

"Are you still interested?"

She stopped and stared. "What?"

"Are you still interested in him?" he said. "It's obvious that you guys were close before. I just wondered if that's still there."

"I don't know," she said. "I literally saw him for the first time today."

"But you should know," he said, "because, like I said, it was very obvious to me that you already had a thing."

"We had a thing," she said, "yes, but we don't still have a thing."

"But you could," he said, staring at her with that same intensity that she'd come to recognize when he needed an answer.

"We might," she said, "but I have no idea because I don't really know how he feels about me now. I don't know if we have that same bond."

"Maybe. Have you discussed me with him?" he asked

with that same studied indifference that she recognized and that he was trying rather hard to ignore.

"Outside of the fact that you are his son and having to explain how and why—which I did explain all that to him—we talked a little bit about you," she said, "but that doesn't mean that we discussed anything in the past right now. I think I gave him an awful lot to think about. He'd also been shot. He's dealing with a pretty rough scenario here presently, and I don't think he's terribly impressed with anything in life right now."

"I guess it's a bit of a shock, isn't it?" he said. "Finding that you've got a son?"

"He was upset that he had missed so much of your life, how he didn't get to be there for the time you were born or your first birthday or your fifth birthday," she said with her hands out, palms up. "And, of course, that just made me feel worse."

"Well, it shouldn't," he said fiercely. "You did everything you could."

"And I agree I did," she said, "but I didn't let him in the process."

Jeremy nodded slowly. "It's one thing to make his own decision to have nothing to do with me. It's another thing when that choice was taken away from him."

She slowly nodded. "Yes," she said, "that's about it."

"Well," he murmured, "the troubled webs we weave." Then he looked at her and asked, "Is dinner ready yet?"

She rolled her eyes and said, "No, not yet, it's early."

"I'm hungry," he complained, and he returned to the fridge, pulled out more pepperoni sticks, and said, "I'll go back to Frank's."

"Fine," she said quietly, knowing that it was his way of

going off to deal with his own problems. "Dinner will be ready in an hour and a half."

"Make it an hour," he said. "Like, I'm really hungry." And he waggled his eyebrows and left.

She stood in the doorway and watched him race down the road. Tears were in her eyes, but they were good tears. Kurt might not have been there for all the milestones with Jeremy, but she had been. And she had done a damn good job as a mom. And Jeremy was a hell of a good son. She was so grateful to have him in her life.

###

LATER THAT EVENING, Kurt picked up the phone and called her personal cell phone number.

"How did you get this number?" she asked sleepily.

"Sorry. I didn't think that you might be in bed this early."

"It's been a pretty tough day. How is the shoulder?" She bolted awake at the thought.

"It's fine," he said, reassuring her. "And I don't know why I called. Guess I needed to hear your voice."

"Well, that's an interesting thought," she said. "After thirteen years of not hearing my voice, *now* you need to hear it?"

"Yeah," he said, "I did. I had so many questions and so many thoughts all day long. They just kept running around in circles in my head."

"You and me both. I told him."

"You told Jeremy?"

"Yes," she said. "I told him. He actually guessed."

"Really?"

"He's not stupid. He put two and two together."

"So not too many people in your life since then, huh?"

"No," she said with a laugh, "and that's pretty well how he figured it out."

"Was he upset?" he asked cautiously.

"Only when I said that you were feeling a bit betrayed."

"And he was upset?"

"He was upset that you would judge me for it."

"Good," he said, "because nobody should judge you for that. Nobody was there to hold your hand or to help you out. You made the best decisions you could at the time under those circumstances, and nobody can fault you for that."

She snorted. "Plenty of people have," she said. "Starting with those who judged me for even dating you or getting pregnant in the first place. Although I didn't tell anybody, everybody assumed it was the no-good lazy bum who had already taken off on me."

"Well, that was partly correct," he said. "I was always a hard worker but not necessarily one who stuck around, was I?" he said.

"How are you feeling about the whole thing now?" she asked cautiously.

"I'm feeling better," he said. "I'll head out to the truck stop early in the morning. Will you be at the coffee shop?"

"I often stop there in the morning, yes. Why?"

"I just thought I could meet you there," he said, "have a morning coffee with you."

"That would be nice," she said warmly. "I'll be there somewhere around seven-thirty."

"Good," he said. "I'll be there quite a bit earlier because I want to see if I can catch the dog early."

"Got it."

"See you in the morning." And he hung up. As he sat here on the edge of his motel room bed, he took off his shirt. His sore and bandaged shoulder kept throbbing. Still, a smile was on his face. She'd always done that to him. He forgot how much he missed it, missed her. Back then they were a twosome—a special twosome—but always knowing that their time apart was rapidly approaching.

It was hard to look back on those years, but he needed to move forward because moving backward wasn't possible. All he could hope was that he had a chance to rekindle a relationship with her and a chance to get to know the son he didn't know he had. And, with that, he rolled over, stretched out on top of the bedding, and turned out the light. He had already checked in with Badger and updated him on everything, including Kurt's new family.

For the moment everybody was quite content. All he could hope was that Sabine was somewhere safe and that she would hold on until he got there. He didn't want to get sidetracked by the rest of this personal stuff; it was too important to make sure that Sabine was taken care of and had a safe place to go. But, at the same time, he also needed to make it all work together, not just one or the other.

He'd lost enough already.

He didn't dare lose any more.

CHAPTER 5

LAURIE ANN WOKE up the next morning, showered, dressed, and was in the kitchen, staring out the glass doors, when, behind her, she heard the sleepy voice of Jeremy.

"Are you meeting him?"

She turned slowly to look at him. "Yes," she said, "we'll meet for coffee."

He nodded slowly, as if contemplating it. "I thought about it a lot last night."

"And?"

She really didn't know what kind of relationship she and Kurt had at the moment, but she was willing to keep the lines of communication open. She also refused to accept any blame. Life happened, and this was just one more example where it happened the way people hadn't expected it to. She'd never regretted her decision and wouldn't start now.

"I'd like to meet him," he said.

"You mean, more than you have?"

He nodded. "I'd like to spend time with him."

"Fine," she said. "I think he'd be happy to hear that."

His gaze held an expression of almost swift relief at her words, and she realized just how much Jeremy was hoping that he wouldn't be rejected. "He didn't know about you," she said quietly. "So there's no rejection on his part."

"Of course there is," he said with the wave of his hand. "I can handle it."

She kept her quiet smile to herself. "I'll mention it to him. Do you want me to invite him over for the weekend?"

He looked at her in surprise. "You mean, for dinner or something?"

"Or even just coffee, if you want to start small."

He thought about it and then said, "He might as well come for a meal. At least then it won't feel quite so awkward."

"Bonding over a meal is an age-old tradition," she said with a bright smile.

"Can I bring Frank?"

She thought about it and realized that he was looking for support outside of her. Feeling a small twinge, she nodded. "I think that works," she said. "How about burgers for four on Saturday?"

"That works," he said. "Now I'm going back to bed."

"I'm leaving soon. Have a good day," she called out.

"You too, Mom." And, with that, he disappeared upstairs. She tossed back the rest of her coffee, picked up her purse, and walked out the door. She didn't know what the future held, but she could feel her son trying to find his way. But then so was she. With any luck so was Kurt. Nobody had answers to this mess. No matter how much they tried, there just wasn't a perfect right or wrong answer in this scenario.

When she arrived at the coffee shop twenty minutes later, she wasn't surprised to find him already sitting at a table against the window. He lifted his hand in acknowledgment, just to show her where he was seated. She walked toward him, the waitress already meeting her partway with the coffeepot.

She smiled and said, "Yes, please," as she took her seat across from Kurt. After the waitress left, Laurie Ann asked, "How's the shoulder?"

"It's better," he said. He gave a casual shrug with the other shoulder but kept that injured one still.

She studied him for a long moment. "Do you always have to be a tough guy?"

He laughed. "Goes with the territory."

"Maybe," she said, unconvinced. "I wanted to invite you for burgers tomorrow night, Saturday," she clarified, "at the house." She watched the surprise and then the joy light up his face.

"I'd be delighted." Then he hesitated and asked, "Does Jeremy know?"

"Yes, and he would like to spend some time with you."

"Good," he said. "I'd like to get to know him."

"I don't know how much one gets to know anybody in a short time frame," she joked, "but it's a start."

"And starts are all we have."

She smiled. "You used to say the darnedest things sometimes," she said. "You'd get all philosophical, and I'd wonder who this person was, sitting beside me, and then you would revert back to being just you."

"It's always just me," he said, chuckling. "Every once in a while though, I'd start wondering about life, the universe, and what the heck we're meant to do with our time here."

"Well, if you ever find out," she said, "please let me know."

"Don't you ever wonder if you're on the right path?"

"All the time," she said, "but my goals were ones I felt I needed to do right from the beginning. So, having made it this far, I can't say I'm unhappy with where I'm at in life."

"No," he said, "I'm in the same boat. I wish I had skipped out on the accident and that I was still in the navy. I expected to be a career seaman, but life happened."

"And you have to find something to replace it now," she said.

The waitress returned with menus and topped up their coffees and left again.

Laurie Ann looked up at him. "Do you have any news on the War Dog?"

"No," he said. "I stopped here last night on my way home, but it was noisy, noisy enough to scare off Sabine. A large group of people had what looked like barbecues going at several trucks on the tailgates. They were settled in, even though the truck stop owners didn't appear to be too happy about it."

"Ah, well, it's not exactly what you would call a tailgate party, but maybe they were traveling through and didn't really have a place to go."

"Maybe. I thought I caught sight of the gang of kids as well," he said, "but, when I headed in their direction, they scattered."

"So it may have been them?"

"May have been. Yes, I did send Amos a text about it."

"You told him that you got shot?"

He gave her a lopsided grin. "Nope, I didn't. Do you think he would believe me or would he just put me in the troublemaker category again?"

"It's been thirteen years," she protested. "Surely every kid's allowed to grow up."

"No, I don't think so," he said. "Small towns, once you are tarred and feathered with a certain brush, I don't think they see you any differently."

"That would be sad," she said. "Everybody deserves a second chance."

"Maybe, I certainly think so, but obviously your parents don't."

"I know," she said, "but that's their loss. They have no relationship with Jeremy either."

"Does he ask about them?"

"He did at first, but I told him the truth, and now he doesn't ask anymore."

"Good," he said, "he's learning."

"These are hard lessons though," she said.

"They are, but those are the lessons that you and I both had to learn too."

"I know." She stared moodily out the window. "You always want to protect your kids, but it seems like there's nothing that you can do to stop them from getting hurt, no matter how hard you try."

"And I'm not sure we have that right," he said slowly. "When you think about it, it's usually through being hurt that we grow."

Her smile peeped out. "There you go with that philosophical stuff again."

"Yeah, sometimes," he said, "but just think about it. I wouldn't be who I am now if I hadn't gone into the navy. It wasn't easy, but I went there eagerly, knowing that it was the right thing for me. Maybe I knew I would end up with a bullet between my eyes pretty damn fast if I didn't change. I don't know. What one does has consequences. But what would have been the consequences if we hadn't gone ahead and done what we did? Imagine if you and I hadn't come together? Jeremy wouldn't exist."

"I know," she said. "I thought about that a lot while I was struggling to pay the bills."

"Ouch," he said, "and I can only tell you that I would have been more than happy to help out."

"And I think I was also being somewhat stubborn and trying hard to do it on my own, as if I wanted to prove to my parents that I didn't need them either."

"And that's pride," he said. "I understand that one fully."

"Not too many would," she said with a smile. "My sister didn't. She thought I was being willfully difficult."

"She was pretty difficult back then, as I recall."

"Yeah, she was, but I still love her. She is my sister, and I love her even more because, even though she didn't approve and didn't agree with my decision, she sucked it all in and helped me out anyway."

"And your parents still have nothing to do with you and Jeremy?"

"No, not really. Every once in a while there's a phone call to make sure I'm alive on the planet. I still send them emails for their birthdays, but I don't do anything more than that."

"The fact that you even do that much," he said, "is amazing, given the hardships they've put you through."

"They didn't put me through anything," she said firmly. "I'm the one who got myself in this condition, and I'm the one who refused to go down their suggested pathway."

"Well, you didn't get there alone," he said, "and I'm sure they have absolutely zero interest in seeing me, but I will try not to hold it all against them."

"You don't need to," she said. "Jeremy's thirteen now, and we're doing just fine."

"You're doing more than fine," he said warmly. "I'm very impressed."

She shook her head. "I don't know why," she said. "He can be a handful sometimes, but he's a good kid."

"And that's what you have to hang on to during the next four, five years. Could be interesting, but, as long as you never regret the decision you made, then that's all that counts."

"How can I regret it?" she asked. "He was the reason I kept going. Because of him I went to med school, following that dream. Back then I thought it was for me, but I also realized I couldn't give him anything if I didn't get a better education."

"You're also blessed," he said with a smile, "to be absolutely brilliant. Not everybody could have made it through med school while raising a child."

"I am lucky," she said. "School was always easy, although med school was a bit of a challenge."

"A bit?" He shook his head. "Most people would be screaming at you right now for that comment."

She chuckled. "I know, and I did have some people who weren't very happy with me finding med school somewhat easy," she said with a shrug. "It's a good thing it was easy because I don't know if I would have made it otherwise. Keeping up all the studies and the exams, along with the demands of having a child, wasn't easy. A couple other moms and dads were in my school. We tended to hang out, as we understood exactly the problems we were all facing. I was the only single parent though, and yet, because of my sister, I was doing almost better than they were."

"Right, because a marriage can be a hardship to try to not blame the other person for."

"Well, my sister already blamed me, so that was an easy one," she said with a shrug. "But she was always there. When I needed a babysitter, she was a live-in babysitter. When I needed shopping done or groceries brought, she would stop and pick up stuff on her way home. We had two rooms in her house, almost like a suite but not quite. We shared the kitchen with her. She couldn't be bothered to cook most of the time, preferring takeout, so that left the kitchen pretty well for me. I couldn't afford the takeout, and I wouldn't ask her for it. She was already keeping a roof over our heads without collecting a dime. Going to med school was already enough of a financial strain," she said. She shook her head, looked at him, and said, "So enough about all of that. What about you? Where do you go from here?"

"Well, life's looking up apparently," he said. "I have a date for dinner on Saturday. I can't remember the last time I went for a barbecue like that."

"I'm sure you always had dates," she scoffed. "You were an incredibly well-loved man when you were here. I'm sure it was the same in the navy."

He laughed. "Well, let's just say, an awful lot of willing females were in our high school. But, once I met *the one*, I never did stray." He looked up at her, frowned, and said, "You know that, right?"

She nodded slowly. "It's one of the things I never doubted, never questioned about you."

"Good," he said with a note of satisfaction.

"I don't think anybody else around me believed it though," she said.

He winced. "No. I'm sure they didn't. It was much easier for everybody to blame me for all the ills that went around in the world and make me look even worse than I actually was."

"You also played into that," she accused him. "You loved that everybody thought you were such a badass."

"I was a badass," he said in protest.

She burst out laughing. "You were, indeed," she said. "Now how about the dog?"

"Well, I got the staff here to agree to call me whenever they see any sign of her," he said, "and I'll meet Amos again in about an hour," he said, looking at his watch.

She glanced down at hers and sighed. "And I'm off to work. I never did order breakfast." She gathered up her purse to pull out some money for the coffee.

He reached a hand out and said, "Coffee's on me."

She smiled. "Thank you." She stood and, with one last look, said, "Don't get into trouble, huh?"

He smiled back and said, "Well, if I do, I know where to come to get patched up again."

She shook her head. "Please don't," she said. "I had a lot of nightmares last night about you as it is."

"Nightmares?" he protested. "You're supposed to dream about me—but not like that."

She burst out laughing and was still grinning when she made her way to her car and later into her office. One thing about the relationship with him, he'd always had the ability to make her smile. And a whole lot of worse things were in life than that, she reminded herself.

KURT WAS JUST finishing his coffee, thinking about what to do for the next hour before his meeting with the detective, when his phone rang.

"Hey, it's Jim down at the truck stop," his caller said. "I think I just saw the dog in the back corner here."

"I'm here already," Kurt said. "Where are you right now?"

"I'm in the back section, doing inventory," he said. "I just saw a huge golden dog. So, if you hurry, she'll still be around."

Kurt got into his truck and pulled in to the back and headed around to the gas station area, and Jim stood there, staring in the distance. Kurt parked beside him, hopped out, and shook his hand. "Thanks for the call," he said.

Jim pointed into one of the thicker areas of the brush. "I swear to God she was just there a few minutes ago."

"Good," he said. "Let me see if I can talk to her."

He headed back to the truck, picked up the leash and a collar, and filled his pockets full of treats. Jim watched as Kurt walked calmly toward the thickest part of the brush and slipped in, away from any watchful eyes. Once out of sight, he called out for her. "Sabine, I'm here. I'm so sorry that you've had such a rough time, but I'm here, little one."

He retraced his steps, moving slowly, heading toward the same tree trunks where he had placed some treats before. As he hit every tree, all the treats were gone, although he realized that the birds could have taken them. Yet he'd like to think it was a good sign that Sabine maybe got some too. He quickly refilled three of the spots closest to the building. He didn't want to put her in any conflict with humans, but he needed to know where she was spending all her time. Then he sat down on one of the fallen logs on the far side and waited.

He heard the rustle of bushes around him, and he completely ignored them, content to just be. He waited, calling her calmly and quietly, telling her that he was here to help make her life a little bit easier and that any time she was ready to come and meet him, he was good with that. His only tool was the sound of his own voice, but she would recognize it fairly quickly and wasn't one that she would know from her recent history, but life wasn't always just about negatives.

After a good twenty minutes, he heard more rustling.

He smiled, put out a hand with some more treats, tossed a few into a pathway that he had been staring at, wondering if she would come close enough to take them. So far he had yet to catch a glimpse of her. He wasn't even sure that it was the right dog he was looking for. But, as he turned around, a pair of glowing eyes were behind a bush.

"It's okay, sweetie. I'm here."

And that might have been enough for him, but it wasn't enough for Sabine. She sat there, staring at him. He was an unknown, and she'd already come up against some ugly unknowns. He tossed some food her way; she looked down at it and then back at him and didn't move.

"And that's a good thing," he said. "You take your time. I'm not here to hurt you. I'm here to save you. We'll get you out of this mess."

And he studied her golden markings to match her up with the pictures he had. It didn't matter if it was the right dog or not because he would make sure that this one was looked after too, but he wanted to make sure that he caught the right one as well. He sat here and waited, right up to the time of his meeting with Amos, telling Sabine that he had to go. When he stood, she disappeared. He immediately put down more treats for her and said, "I'll be back in an hour or so." When he walked back to the truck stop, the detective stood out front, talking on his phone.

Amos hung up, looked at Kurt, and asked, "Now what?"

"I don't know," Kurt said in a calm voice. "You wanted to meet me."

"Somebody said they heard gunshots here."

"Well, one for sure," Kurt said in a calm voice.

"Did you fire it?"

"No, sure didn't."

"Are you armed?"

"No, I'm not," he said.

The detective looked at Kurt's rental truck and looked at him suspiciously.

Kurt stepped back and said, "Go ahead and search it."

Amos frowned and then shook his head. "Did you see the shooter?"

"I think so, yes, but I didn't see the shooter in the act to know for sure," he said. "I think it was one of the punk kids in that five-person gang who hangs around here."

At that, the detective's face wrinkled up. "They've been nothing but trouble," he said. "I keep hoping that something will change, and either I can nail their asses to the wall and put them in jail or they'll turn a new leaf and become decent human beings."

"How long have they been doing this?" Kurt asked.

"Years. One of them is nothing but trouble." He slid a sideways look at Kurt. "Kind of like you."

"Well, I turned out okay," he said easily.

"Maybe, maybe not. The jury's still out on that one."

"Right," he said, fully realizing that what he had said to Laurie Ann was so true. Once tarred by a certain brush, it was hard to assume a different image. "Still everybody deserves a second chance," he said.

"And some of them are just bad through and through," the detective growled. He stared off in the distance. "So what do you know about the gunfire?"

"I know it was aimed at me," he said.

"Did it hit you?"

He gave him a lopsided glance. "Just slightly."

The detective's gaze narrowed. "He shot you?"

"Yeah, took a burn on the shoulder," he said, pulling over his T-shirt collar, so Amos could see the bandage.

"And you didn't report it?"

"No," he said, "I'm not exactly the most desirable person to be reporting things like that."

The detective started swearing at him.

Kurt held up a hand. "Stop," he said. "The days where I have to listen to that shit are long gone. I made a decision not to go to the hospital, not to press charges. It's just a flesh wound, and it's not bad."

"And how are we supposed to ever deal with these kids," he said, "if we don't catch them after crap like this?"

"Well, if I could have caught him," he said, "I would have. Believe me. I'm still looking for him."

At that, the detective froze and glared. "No vigilante justice."

"I didn't say it would be," he stated, reining in his own temper. But it's obvious the detective didn't believe him. Kurt blew out a long breath. "I know you've still got a problem with me," he said. "The fact is, back then, you had a reason, but you don't now. I'm a completely different person. You don't have to believe me. I don't really care, but I don't want to get shot any more than you want to get shot," he said. "You can dig the bullet out of the seat of my truck, if you want."

"Well, if you don't report this, I can't pull the kids in for it."

"Who are these five kids?"

"Well, they're prime pickings for one of the local gangs," he said, "who is actively recruiting new members right now."

Kurt winced. "They have to keep the numbers up."

"The gang wars have gotten much worse since you left," the detective said. "Some of it's pretty ugly stuff."

"It was always ugly stuff," he said. "It's just a matter of time before the ugliness gets younger and younger."

"It's here now," Amos said. "They're pulling in a lot of teens—fourteen, fifteen, sixteen-year-old kids."

"And that's not cool," Kurt said, thinking about his own son, Jeremy.

"Well, sometimes they get them into these situations, where the kids don't know how to get out of it. So they end up in the gang, even though they didn't want to," he said. "But, once they're hooked, they're pressured to stay or are blackmailed into staying, and that just becomes a bad end all the way around."

"You can't do anything about it?"

"We're trying," he said, "but our hands are hampered by the law."

"Of course they are," he said. "Off the record, having just found out I have a thirteen-year-old son," he said, "I wouldn't be happy at all to find out that he was forced into a similar situation."

"No, of course not. None of us want our families involved. But too often it's the families busily working hard to put food on the table who have lost control of their kids. The parents have no idea what their kids are doing during the day, and, once it starts going sideways, it's pretty hard to pull it back."

Kurt thought about that for a long moment, his face grim, as he realized just how lucky Jeremy was to have Laurie Ann as his mom. Then Kurt wondered just how much control or knowledge of what Jeremy was up to that Laurie Ann had. "If you know who they are, why haven't you picked them up?"

"On what charge?" Amos asked. "So far they haven't committed a crime."

"Except shooting me."

"Well, I don't know anything about that shooting, now do I?" the detective said sarcastically. "Because some asshole forgot to file a complaint."

"Well, that's because this asshole has been on the receiving end too many times," he said, "so he didn't figure he'd get a fair shot or that anybody would even listen to him."

The detective stopped, glared at him, and said, "Well, you would have. We have to look after criminals too, you know?"

"Sure," he said, "but who's the priority here? I wouldn't put in a complaint to have it ignored. I'd be much better off if I do something myself."

"And that's what I don't want you to do," the detective snapped. "Again, no vigilante justice."

"I didn't say anything about that," he said, "but, if the gang is hooking up innocent kids, that's not cool."

"Doesn't matter if it's cool or not. It's none of your business," he said. "You stay out of it, unless you're a cop."

"Well, I hadn't considered going into law enforcement," he said, "but you never know."

With that, the detective shook his head and said, "Don't bother. Your history is against you."

"No, not true," he said. "I'm an adult now, and I have a hell of a lot of good references in recent history to take me where I need to go now."

"Yeah, did you buy them?" Amos asked with a sneer, as he hopped into his vehicle, not giving Kurt a chance to say anything. The detective took off driving down the road, obviously pissed at the world.

While that was okay with Kurt, Amos could be pissed all he wanted. These kids though? Well, they deserved to have their clocks cleaned at least once to realize what they were up against. Kurt didn't know if that would have helped him when he was that age or not. He'd been too cocky and sure of himself, but he hadn't shot anybody or even attempted to. Something was going down, and he didn't want to get involved in local gang issues, but they'd already involved him. So he didn't really see that he had a whole lot of choice. And that would just put him up crossways with the law all over again. So maybe he wasn't all that different now.

Some things just seemed to never change.

CHAPTER 6

AT NOON THE receptionist walked into Laurie Ann's office and said, "You look beat."

Laurie Ann looked up, smiled, and said, "Well, I guess I feel a little bit better than that." She looked at her watch, shook her head, and asked, "Where did the morning go?"

"You have to be at your other clinic in about an hour, right?"

"Two hours," she said, "if the flooding has been controlled and if they're accepting patients again. They were supposed to call me but ..." She pulled up her phone and checked and said, "I'm not seeing any messages." She quickly phoned the other clinic, only to find out that the repair work was still being carried out. So she had a second afternoon off in a row. She smiled and said, "I know I shouldn't be so happy to have an afternoon off again," she said, "but it really is a treat."

"Go home and do something fun," she said. "You don't have to stay here. All your clients are gone."

"Yeah, that's good," she said, "but it also feels weird." She grabbed her purse and walked out to her car. She thought about whether she should detour to the truck stop. She wanted to know if Kurt was back there again and if he'd made any headway with the dog. It was an impulse that she found irresistible, turning in the direction of the coffee shop, where she'd met him earlier.

She pulled into the parking lot on the far side twenty minutes later and smiled when she saw his truck. She parked beside it and hopped out, but she saw no sign of him. She frowned at that and walked around to the other side and headed into the coffee shop again. Again, there was no sign of him, but then he could be anywhere. She walked back outside and stood there, looking around for a long moment but again found nothing. She frowned, picked up her phone, and called him.

When he answered, she said, "Well, I'm parked beside your truck, at least I think it's yours," she said, walking back over to it, "but where are you?"

"I'm in the bush," he said, his voice quiet. "I'm trying to connect with a little lady back here."

"Did you find her?" she asked in delight.

"Well, I think so, but she's deliberately being a shadowy figure. I can't get close enough to see her clearly."

"Well, I don't expect anybody would bond very quickly," she said. "Trust takes time."

"Absolutely it does," he said in a warm tone. "Anyway I'll be there in a few minutes."

"I don't want to disturb you," she said. "If you need to stay there and work with her a bit, I can go on home."

"I'll come say hi to you," he said. "Be out in a minute."

With that, she put away her phone, walked closer to his truck, leaned against the tailgate, and waited for him. Hearing sounds off to the side, she looked to see a bunch of kids, then revised her opinion from kids to young adults coming toward her. Five of them. They all wore identical sneers on their face. She looked at the leader and frowned. "Can I help you?"

"Is this your truck?" he asked, motioning at Kurt's truck.

She shook her head. "No, it's not."

"You're leaning against it."

"Yeah," she said. "Is there a law against that?" She wasn't sure what she was getting into, but just something about his attitude bothered her. She looked closer at his buddies and asked one of the kids, "Hey, aren't you Reggie?"

"How do you know who I am?"

"You're a couple years ahead of my son," she said, "Jeremy."

"Jeremy?" He frowned and then nodded. "Big kid?"

"Yep, big kid," she said with a bright smile. "I think you guys were on the same basketball team or something."

He looked sideways at his buddies.

"Nah, basketball's lame," the leader said, twirling a piece of bar in his hand.

She turned to face him, looked at the bar, looked at the kid, and asked, "What are you doing carrying around that pipe?"

"None of your business," he said.

She nodded slowly. "So why are you standing here with me?" she asked. "Just so I understand what it is that you're planning on doing."

"Well, we were planning on beating the hell out of the truck," the leader said with a sneer.

But Reggie turned and looked at him. "No, we aren't," he said. "We're just leaving." He tried to drag his friend away.

"Fuck that shit," the bar-swinging leader snapped, pulling free.

"Is this what you do with your life?" she asked. "You attack vehicles parked here?" She knew the amazement in her voice was a little overdone, but she was struggling to understand how somebody like Reggie—who'd seemed to have so many good things going for him in his life—was here with this group. She looked at Reggie. "Is this what you do with your spare time?"

"No," he said, but the other kids crowded closer and said, "Yes."

"So which is it?" she asked, looking from one to the other.

"It's none of your business what it is, bitch," the leader said. Reggie frowned and took half a step forward, almost protectively, as the other guy said, "Don't even fucking play games with me now. You know what we came here to do."

"Yeah, but she wasn't supposed to be here."

And Laurie Ann realized that they knew who owned this truck, and she was literally in the wrong place at the wrong time. "So hang on a minute. You're trying to beat up the truck, or is it the guy who drives this truck that you're trying to attack?"

"Why? You sleeping with him?" the smart-ass kid said.

She shook her head slowly. "No," she said. "But I sure as hell wouldn't want to get on the wrong side of him."

"Yeah, and why not?" he asked.

"Well, for one, he's a war vet, and the world doesn't take it kindly when you start beating up war heroes," she said. "Two, he's from around here and is fairly well-known, although he's been gone for more than ten years."

"I don't give a fuck who he is," he said. "The guy's a drip, and he pissed me off, so he'll pay for it."

"So you're some big tough dude, and this guy pissed you off?" She didn't even know where her bravado was coming from because it's obvious that these kids were out for trouble, and it didn't matter where. These kids would cause trouble.

"Yeah, and now you're pissing me off," he said, turning the bar toward her.

"What are you doing? You plan to attack an innocent woman, standing here, not hurting anyone. Is that who you are?" She couldn't believe what she'd gotten herself into. How long would Kurt take to get here?

"Fuck, yeah," he said, "that's who I am." He swung his arm back, when Reggie grabbed it and said, "No, that's not who we are. We don't go attacking women who were just talking to us. What's wrong with you, man?"

But the leader turned around and whaled on Reggie hard with the bar. "Don't you fucking talk to me like that," he said, "and don't you ever talk to me like that in front of somebody else."

Reggie's face twisted in pain, but the attack had been effective, as he pulled back, holding his shoulder. "It's still wrong," he insisted.

At that, the punk leader stepped forward, raising the bar, as if to hit him again, and Reggie took several more steps back, and she saw the fear in his face.

"You know, Reggie, that you don't have to hang around with guys like this," she said. "They are heading down a path you don't want to go."

He looked at her and shook his head. "It's all right."

"I don't think so," she said. "You can get out of this."

No," he said, "I don't think I can."

"You're fucking right he can't," the punk leader said, turning back on her. "And you need a lesson yourself."

"Yeah, and you're the guy who'll do it, huh?"

"You're fucking right, bitch," he said. "By the time we're

done with you, you'll be begging for us to kill you."

Hearing a single soft footstep behind her, she said, "Well, you could try that, but I really don't think that's a wise move."

The gang leader looked at her in stunned amazement. "You fucking daring me to do it?" And he swung the bar back again, his face twisting in fury. The other three guys—two of them with maniac grins and wide dilated eyes on either side of the leader—nudged forward with their leader, but Reggie stepped back. And she noted something else out of the corner of her eyes.

Just then Kurt stepped in front of her, grabbed the bar, and smacked the punk hard across the shoulder. She could hear the bone take a hell of a blow, and then Kurt turned the bar on the other three punks and dropped them to the ground. The four young men stared up at him in shock.

Reggie turned and bolted, but she knew where to find him.

The punk leader was screaming about his shoulder as he jumped to his feet, barreling his head into Kurt's chest and stomach area, but Kurt raised his knee and smashed his jaw hard. Once the punk was down on the ground again and groaning, blood spurting from his jaw and his nose, Kurt turned to look at her with a hard gaze. "You okay?"

Shaky, she nodded and pressed her fingers to her temples. "I am," she said, "but I don't know what the hell's going on with the world. Is this what we have for kids nowadays?"

Kurt pulled out his phone, made a phone call, while she stared at the kids on the ground. The two who seemed high on drugs were unconscious, as was the third. The fourth one, the foul-mouthed leader, was probably wishing he was knocked out because he still screamed in pain.

"Do you know the kid who got away?" Kurt asked.

She hated to answer this one, but she nodded and said, "Yes, his name's Reggie. He's two years ahead of Jeremy in school. They were on the same basketball team for a while."

Kurt passed the name off to whoever was on the other end of the phone. When he put away the phone, he said, "The cops will be here in a few minutes."

And she took a long slow deep breath. "I'd just as soon avoid that."

"Can't now," he said. "I tried to avoid it myself. But, with this punk here coming back for another lesson, returning for a second round, we need to bring the law into it."

"Fucking asshole," said the punk, who just poured out more obscenities nonstop.

Kurt looked at her and said, "You know what? If you weren't here, I'd have shut that kid's mouth a long time ago."

She nodded. "I appreciate the restraint."

"Makes no sense to me," he said. "A mouth like that needs to be taught a lesson."

"You don't think this would be a big-enough lesson?"

"No."

KURT HOOKED AN arm around her shoulders and tucked her up close, dropping a kiss on her temple.

Laurie Ann wrapped her arms around him and hugged him tight. "I was really scared," she murmured. "The only reason I even stayed on my feet was I knew you were on the way."

"And I was here," he said. "I was maneuvering into a better position, where I could take him out."

"Well, I'm glad you didn't just kill him outright," she said with half a smile.

"Should have," he said. "Once he heads down this pathway, it gets ugly."

"You were never this bad," she said, hearing something in his tone.

He looked down, smiled, kissed her forehead gently, and said, "Maybe not, but I don't know that I was far from it."

"The gangs are supposed to be much worse now," she said, as she looked down at the kids. "What will happen to them?"

"I'm not sure," he said. "Unfortunately probably nothing."

She stared at him in shock.

"They didn't attack you, did they?"

"Well, they surrounded me and tried to attack me, but you stopped them."

"And that will make a bit of a difference, but, if it's a first offense, they will probably get off with a warning."

"That's scary," she said. "I don't want to be around this area of town then."

"And unfortunately one of them knows you and Jeremy, right?"

"Yes, and where we live then," she said, a shiver passing along her spine.

"Yeah," he said. "Not good."

In the distance they heard the sirens. Two cop cars pulled up, and the detective was among them. Amos walked over, two more cops with him, took one gander at the four on the ground, turned toward Kurt with a hard look, and asked, "So you attacked them?"

"Hell no," Laurie Ann said, stepping forward, anger in her voice. "They surrounded me, intent on attacking me with those pipes. Kurt stepped in to defend me."

Amos looked at her in surprise. "Seriously?" The pair of cops with him looked on, silent.

She nodded and explained what had happened.

Amos shook his head, looked down at the kids, pried open their eyes, and checked their vitals. "These two are too high to tell us anything and likely won't even remember what happened," he said.

"You can check with Reggie," she said. "He was the other guy here, but he got popped for sticking up for me and left."

"You had another one too?"

"The fifth one, he's two years ahead of my son in school. And when Reggie tried to stop the gang leader from attacking me, the leader turned that nasty bar against him. I don't know how badly hurt Reggie is, but, when the leader threatened me again, Reggie tried to interfere. I told him that he needed to get clear of this crap, and he said he didn't think he could get out of the deal now anyway."

"And that's what I mean," Amos said, the two cops nodding. "These gangs get into the kids' lives and make it impossible for them to get out."

"How though?" Laurie Ann asked.

"It's hard to say for sure, but they find a way to blackmail them or to get them to do something either illegal or that they're ashamed of or something the gang will then hold over their heads, until they've got them where they want them. Once they start doing major crimes, there's no going back anyway."

"What's this then?" she said, motioning to the gang members on the pavement. "Is this just nothing then?"

"No, this is a major crime at this point, but we've also only got your word for it that they attacked you and that you're not sitting here defending him," he said with a head nod toward Kurt.

She stared at Amos in shock. "Seriously?" She faced the other two cops. "What about you two?"

But they remained silent, glancing at Amos.

"Sure, you were in his arms when we got here. You would do anything to defend him," he said. "We've seen that time and time again."

Kurt felt his stomach sink. "That may be," he said, "but that is not the way it happened, and you're not even trying to protect her from these thugs. You're just trying to get me in trouble."

"No," he said, "I'm looking at this as a cop who arrived to see you holding her with four guys at your feet."

"I see," she said faintly. "So it's really more important for you to nail Kurt's ass after all these years than it is for you to get justice for me, is that it?"

"If we find out that what really happened is as you said it was, that's a different story." He shrugged. "But we'll need proof first."

Again the two silent cops with Amos nodded.

"Did you ever think that maybe cameras are here?" she asked Amos in a hard voice.

Kurt turned to look at her and could see the anger in her eyes, and he grinned. "You always were the first one to defend me."

"That's because assholes like Amos were all too eager to throw you to the wolves," she snapped, glaring at the detective.

The detective raised his eyebrows at her. "We didn't do anything to him that he didn't deserve."

"Maybe not," she said, "but you made it damn hard for him to change his ways."

Kurt was touched at her need to defend him and reached out a hand and said, "It's okay. I'm not the crazy boy I was way back when," he said, "and this was completely legit self-defense. They surrounded you, about to attack you with a steel bar. There's absolutely no need for the cops to even look at me over this."

"Except," she snapped, glaring at the detective, "they already are. As long as Amos has somebody who's good for this, he won't look to punish the assholes on the ground. He'll just let them create their own little story and have you put in jail."

"Maybe," Kurt said, "except for the cameras here." He pulled out his phone and called Badger. When he explained that he was in a spot of trouble and that he needed camera access on the truck stop, the detective immediately started yelling at him.

"Whoa, whoa, you don't touch those damn cameras."

"Oh, hell, yes," he explained to Badger. "I've got a detective here who wants to pin my ass to the wall instead of the four gang kids who surrounded a woman with steel bars to beat her to a pulp. So the detective is Amos …" And Kurt reeled off his full name and then gave Badger the name and address of the truck stop. When he hung up his phone, he said, "Let's see how you get out of this one. Expect a phone call from US Navy Commander Cross."

"I was doing my job," the detective said in fury.

"No, you weren't. And neither of you were trying to do

anything right either." She turned to look at the two other cops, looking at each other and over at the detective, but who still weren't saying anything. "Even your cronies here will not say anything," she said, "because it's not about the truth for you, is it? It's all about making sure you nail Kurt." She looked pointedly at the two cops and asked, "Do you know this guy?"

They shook their heads.

"He was my boyfriend thirteen years ago. He was a bad boy on a bad track, but he went into the navy. He pulled up stakes, completely changed his life, became a Navy SEAL, and served to protect your sorry asses for thirteen years," she said, with an arm sweep to include Amos. "Then Kurt comes home, does a job for the War Dogs Division that places him here. Five punk kids surround me with steel bars to beat me to a pulp, and Kurt rescues me. And do you guys care?" She shook her head. "You don't."

The silent men finally protested. "Hey, we don't know anything about what happened here. We're still at the beginning of our investigation."

"Yeah, but you listen to him," she said, motioning at Amos, the detective, "and then there won't be an investigation. It'll be a slam dunk, and this poor guy, Kurt, will find his ass in jail. So believe me. I'm watching and so is the rest of the world to see how you handle this."

At that, the detective swore on her. "Don't you even begin to think you'll get into our investigation," he sneered.

"You're the one whose ass is on the line now," she said, leveling him with a hard look. "Kurt here isn't a punk kid anymore. He's got friends in high places, and he's in the right, so you do what's right and make sure that you clean up this gang mess! In the meantime, you need to call an ambulance for the guys bleeding all over the ground."

With his arm around her, Kurt backed her up slightly and said, "Come on. Let's sit you down in your car, until you calm down."

She looked up at him, shook her head, and said, "No, I want a piece of pie and coffee."

He started to chuckle. "I can get behind that idea." He looked back at the other cops. "If and when you're ready to take a statement from us," he said, "we'll be inside." And nudging her gently, he pulled her toward the coffee shop.

As they walked, a golden streak beside him tore off into the woods, and he froze.

"What was that?" she asked.

He called out, "Sabine? Come here, girl."

The dog turned, looked at him, and bolted into the trees.

"Wow," Laurie Ann said. "Was that her?"

"I think so, yes."

"Well, she certainly turned at the sound of your voice."

"But the question is," he said, "what was she doing here in the first place?"

"Maybe she heard the ruckus and was coming to investigate?"

"Maybe," he said. He looked over to the cops, still moving the gang members. "I think she attacked these punks in the first place, which has her life on the line," he said.

"Maybe," she said. "So then I hate these gang members even more."

"Not a whole lot we can do about rescuing her right now. But those kids? That's a whole different story."

"Do you think the cops will do anything?"

"They will give them a warning. Maybe charge them,

then release them on bail. They'll come back after me and possibly you now."

She sucked in her breath. "Seriously?" She froze, looked up at him.

Just then they heard a short bark.

"Do you want to go talk to her?"

He frowned, hesitating, torn between his choices. Then he shook his head firmly and said, "No, let's get you inside to have a coffee."

She stopped, placed a hand on his chest, and said, "I'm fine. I'll go order coffee and pie. You go talk to Sabine and see if you can take a few more steps across that bridge."

And, with that, she turned and walked away. He loved her strong character, who she was, and raced after the dog. When he got to the brush, he sat down on one of the logs and just called out to her, "Come on, girl. Come here." He put a few more treats from his pocket on the log, and, when he turned to look at her, she was there, staring, her eyes wide and glittering.

"Those were the assholes who hurt you, weren't they?"

She gave a small *woof.*

He nodded. "That's all right. I hurt a few of them for you. What I do need to do is make sure they don't know about the connection between you and me. Otherwise they're likely to come back after you," he murmured. And that was not something he was prepared to let happen. He smiled, placed a few more treats there, tossed a few at her feet, and then stood. She immediately backed up into the brush.

"That's all right, girl," he said. "I know it's been a tough life. But it'll get better, I promise."

And, with that, he turned, and he slowly walked away.

When he stopped at the edge of the brush, he smiled, whistled, gave her a wave. "I'll be back tonight," he promised. And he headed back to the coffee shop.

CHAPTER 7

LAURIE ANN WATCHED as Kurt sat down to join her at the booth, her coffee and pie before her to soothe her emotions after the encounter with the pipe-wielding teenage gang. "Did you find Sabine?"

"Yeah, but progress comes in small steps," he said. "I'll come back tonight and visit with her some more."

"Okay," she said, but a note of doubt was in her voice.

When the waitress appeared, he said, "I'll have what she's having. Thank you." He turned and smiled at Laurie Ann. "Trust does not happen overnight."

She nodded. "I know that," she said and frowned. "Do you really think Jeremy or I am in danger from that teenage gang?"

"I don't know. The gang leader will get his broken nose and arm treated, but I have no idea how many other friends he has."

"Because I don't want to think of any harm coming to Jeremy."

"Oh, no, that won't go down well either," he said, studying her face.

"But you're not telling me it's *not* a possibility."

"No," he said. "I never lied to you. Remember?"

She winced. "Great," she said, "so, in effect, this could get very ugly."

"Right now, no reason to even think about that," he said. "With any luck those teenagers have other crimes that they can be held on, and they'll go straight to jail."

"Maybe," she said. "What about Reggie?"

"He's the one who walked away?"

She nodded. "I'm afraid that they'll go after him."

"And it's possible," he said. "Unfortunately there can be no good answers in something like this."

"There's no good answers all around. They're teenagers and already just hoodlums, with guns and pipes," she said in outrage. "And they threatened me when I didn't do anything."

"They didn't care if you did or not. They are belligerent, ugly personalities, looking to make themselves feel better because they hate their lives. The only way to do that is to beat on somebody else," he said. "They needed to pump up who they are to make themselves feel like they are big badasses."

"You were never like that," she said.

"Nope," he said, "because I was already a cocky badass, who knew I was a badass. I didn't have to do stupid stunts like that to feel empowered."

She snorted. "Maybe that's why my parents hated you so much."

"They hated me because they knew I was trying to get into their daughter's pants," he said with a grin.

"Well, you did that," she said, "but why is it everyone believes that I was an innocent party?"

"Because fathers look upon their daughters as being young and innocent. Those fathers know perfectly well that, when they were young themselves, they did things that they weren't very happy with."

She sat back and said, "I was supposed to have a nice afternoon off because the other clinic still isn't back up and running," she said, "and instead I'm emotionally exhausted now."

"I know," he said. "And I'm sorry. It's not how I intended the afternoon to go."

"It's not your fault," she said. "I'm the one who stopped to see if you were here."

"And I like that," he said. "I really do."

She smiled. "And will you come for dinner tonight instead?"

"I thought it was planned for tomorrow night?"

"Yeah, but I'm feeling a little bit uneasy about this whole thing," she said. "I'd feel better if you came tonight too."

"Then I'll come," he said immediately. "Do you want to tell Jeremy ahead of time, so it's not a shock?"

"I suppose I should." She pulled out her phone, looked down, and said, "There's a couple of messages from him anyway."

She scrolled through them, seeing the usual request to stay at Frank's. She looked up at Kurt and said, "He's asking to stay at Frank's tonight."

"Overnight?" he asked.

"It's often what happens."

"You like Frank?"

"He's a good kid," she said, "and, in this world, when I see other punks—like the ones who were just here threatening me—I realize just how good both my teenage son and Frank are."

"So tell him that I'll be there for dinner. He can come join us or not, but otherwise we'll meet tomorrow for the burgers."

She thought about that and then nodded and quickly sent a text. When her son responded with **Why is he coming tonight?** she didn't know what to say. She looked again at Kurt. "He's asking why you are coming tonight."

"Because we want to be together," he said quietly.

She stared at him and could feel some of the tension inside her creeping back in again. "I've haven't really dated since I had him," she said. As Kurt's gaze widened, she nodded. "He was the most important thing in my life. I was in school, and I didn't have a chance to go out very much. I tried a couple dates when he was younger, and that just didn't work out very well, so I avoided the whole dating game."

"So now you don't know what he'll think of it?"

"I guess," she said, slowly working her way through it. "Maybe I'm embarrassed. Maybe I'm just unsure."

"Well," he said quietly, "you'll have to make the call on this one." Kurt watched her curiously to see how she would handle this.

She let out her breath slowly. Then raised her phone and texted her son. **He's coming for dinner because we want to spend time together. You too. Bring Frank.** When no answer came immediately from her son, she said with a wince, "So that may have just killed that conversation."

"What did you say?"

After she told him, she watched the slowest smile grow on his face. "It'll be a lot of adjustment to even have you around for a little while."

"I know," he said. "I was thinking that same thing, but it doesn't mean that we don't deserve to spend time alone with each other as well as a family."

The waitress returned with Kurt's coffee and pie. He

nodded his thank-you to her as she left them alone again.

"Is this really what we want?" she asked, narrowing her gaze at him. "We can't go back in time."

"Good," he said. "Who the hell wants to. I'm very different. You're very different, and there's absolutely no reason at all that we should have to do that."

"Meaning?"

"I like who you are today too," he said honestly, "and I really would like to spend some time with you."

"But, once again, you're not staying around, are you?" she asked quietly. "So, once again, this is short-term, just to connect for a little while, and then you'll be gone."

"I don't know about that," he said. "I haven't made any plans for my future yet, now that I'm out of the navy and mostly rehabbed from my accident. So I don't have a job or a career to offer you," he said.

Her eyebrows rose. "I don't remember saying I needed that offered."

"Maybe not," he said, "but I can just see your parents in the background, frowning with displeasure, because I'm still not a good prospect."

"Sure," she said with a negligent shrug. "But they've been doing that all your life, whether you knew it or not."

He burst out laughing.

She glanced to one of the big windows in the coffee shop and frowned. "But our priority right now needs to be the dog."

He looked outside and frowned. "What is it?"

"I think I saw somebody just go into the bushes where she is," she said.

He scanned the area. "I'll be back in a few minutes."

"Don't worry about me." She shook her head and said,

"Go. I'll head home. I might have a nap. I'm feeling just that tired right now."

"Do you still want me to come for dinner?"

She checked her watch and said, "How about at six?"

"I'll be there," he said. He smiled and added, "I'll go rescue another damsel right now."

And he disappeared.

KURT STRODE OUT of the restaurant and picked up his pace to a light jog, heading in the same direction as he'd seen a man now entering the woods. It could be some guy who just needed to take a leak, but it also happened to be the same area where Sabine was.

Besides, Kurt wasn't at all sure that these five kids, the young gang members, didn't have somebody older behind them. And, if somebody in any gang had something against Sabine, it wouldn't make a damn bit of difference to Kurt. He'd take them down, save the War Dog from further abuse.

As he headed to the shrubbery, he didn't dare look behind him, but he was pretty sure that Laurie Ann stood at the entranceway to the coffee shop, watching him. He stepped into the woods and stopped in silence. He listened, quietly hearing the crunch off to the side—a stealthiness to it that made him frown.

He hoped that Sabine had smarts enough to separate enemy from friend. But then he remembered some of the training that she had had back when she was in the War Dogs program, how she had been trained to sniff out the enemy versus her own trainers. The trouble was, did she understand who was who at this point in her civilian life?

She'd been on her own for a long time, and just enough assholes were out here to confuse her.

Kurt kept moving quietly in the direction of the stranger. As he came to a slight opening, he stepped back under cover and stared. An older man—maybe late forties, early fifties—crouched and studied the trees in front of him. He obviously wasn't here to take a look at nature. Matter of fact, he looked like he was here for nothing but trouble.

Kurt highly doubted the stranger was trying to help Sabine, given the stance he projected. Kurt studied the stranger and waited to see if Sabine would approach. When the stranger pulled a small handgun from his back pocket and raised it, Kurt thrashed around in the undergrowth to chase Sabine away.

The man turned in irritation and looked at him. "What the hell do you want?"

"Well, I didn't know that I wanted anything," he said. "I was just walking around the area ..." Then he saw the gun in his hand, reacting supposedly in shock. "Hey, man, what are you doing?"

The guy waved the gun at him and said, "Get the hell out of here."

"Why? What are you doing with a gun in here?" he asked, raising his voice, as if scared.

The guy sneered. "Why do you want to know?" he asked. "I told you to get lost."

"Or else what?"

The guy stared at him. "Or else I might just use this in your direction."

"What are you planning to shoot?" Kurt continued to play dumb to get more out of the gunman.

"I can hunt mad dog all I want," he said with a sneer.

And that confirmed what Kurt had been afraid of. "You're the one who's been attacking that dog around here?" he said, letting his supposed fear ease down again.

The guy stared at him. "What are you talking about?"

"I heard somebody was out here, abusing a lost dog."

The guy straightened up. "I'm not doing any such thing. That dog is bad news. It needs to be put down."

"Yeah, I can see right now how the dog is attacking you," Kurt said with a smirk. "So you just make up shit to kill dogs?" Kurt said, as if too stupid to understand when he was in trouble. In the meantime, he stared at the guy's stance and realized that the gunman was all bravado, not showing any training.

The guy took several steps toward Kurt, waving the gun at him. "I told you to get the hell away," he snapped. "It's not my fault if you can't learn the lesson."

And he raised his gun, as if to shoot, and immediately Kurt put up his hands, as if to ward off a bullet. "Hey, man, I don't mean any harm."

"Really?" He shook his head. "That's not what I see from my side," he said. "Looks to me like you're up to no good. Now why don't you get the hell away from here."

"I'm going," Kurt said, slowly backing up, "but I can't stand to see anybody hurt a dog."

"Stick around much longer, and you'll see it all right," he said, "because this dog deserves a bullet."

"Why? What she did to you?"

"She hurt one of my associates," he said. "Just a young man who didn't know any better and thought the dog was harmless."

"You mean, one of those five young punks who have been terrorizing the neighborhood?"

At that, the guy cocked his gun and raised it higher. "I don't know who you're talking about, but it better not be about my kids."

And that was enough for Kurt. "Ah, so you're their mentor, their leader. Are you the one who blackmails them into being assholes?"

"No blackmailing required," he said casually, studying Kurt, as if not quite sure if he was a threat or not.

"Well, some of them are definitely bad news," he said, "but not all teenagers are bad."

"They're all bad news," the stranger snapped. "I make sure that they stay that way. No room in this world for wussies."

"Ya think?" Kurt said with a sneer, as he shifted position, waiting for the other man to make a move. The problem was, the stranger would likely react with that gun. Kurt didn't have any K9 training himself to gain Sabine's assistance through standard military orders. But, since finding out what he would be heading into, needing more intel about the dog he was trying to coerce back to a decent life, Kurt wondered if he knew enough to get her to attack or, better yet, to find the enemy, to seek them out, and to take them down. He looked at the old man and said, "What's the matter, old man? You ain't got nothing left in you, so you got to use a weapon?"

At that, he swore. "Don't call me an old man, you piece of shit. You don't even know what it's like to fight," he said. "You're nothing but an ignorant prick."

Kurt smiled at him and said, "So do your worst. Come on. Put that gun down, and show me what you're made of. Everybody seems to think they're a big man when they have a weapon in their hand," Kurt said, taunting his opponent, "but take away that weapon, and they're nothing but a piece of lily-livered fear-struck rubber-necked chicken."

At that, the old man's eyes glittered with hate—and that was the right word for it. There was something so deranged about this character that all the stranger could see through his own fury was the man in front of him and his growing need to punch Kurt's face to the ground.

It was an odd feeling to know that somebody could hate that deeply with so little provocation. Kurt could handle a street fight with this guy, unless the madman got a good shot in, whether with his fists or his gun. Kurt just had to make sure this guy didn't drop Kurt because he knew that there would be no tomorrow for Sabine if that were the case. This kind of guy killed indiscriminately, just like the dog he was hoping to shoot. As far as this old man was concerned, he was law, and whoever crossed him would pay the price.

He smiled a mouthful of rotten teeth and said, "What I'm not is stupid. You're younger, maybe stronger. But you don't have any brains. No way in hell I'm letting go of this gun. I can pop you from here, so you'll never see tomorrow. Why the hell would I put my gun down?"

"I just thought you might like your hands free," he said, watching as Sabine came up behind the stranger, crouching slowly, her teeth bared, not a sound coming from her. And, with the appearance of Sabine, Kurt gave the one solid hand motion he had learned to give a War Dog, and that was to attack. She didn't hesitate. She didn't question the order. She jumped from a standstill, up into a solid six-foot lunge, and grabbed the guy in the shoulder of his gun arm.

He screamed, his jerky trigger finger firing off the gun. One, two, and by the third shot, Sabine had pulled him down and backward. Kurt was on the gunman in a second.

He punched him to knock him out, flipped him over, and pulled his hands behind his back. The bigger struggle was to get the dog to release the gunman's shoulder. But, with the old guy unconscious, Kurt talked Sabine down and finally got her to relax enough to release.

Finally the dog settled down, whining. Kurt dug into his pockets, found some treats, and tossed her one. She immediately gave a thankful *woof.*

"Feels good to get back a little control, doesn't it?" he murmured to Sabine. "The whole world isn't full of assholes, sweetheart, just a large portion of them."

She inhaled the treat.

He added, "We'll work hard to make sure you don't have to come across them again."

And he carefully held out his hand and dropped a few more treats, close by, in front of him. She crouched on her belly to get a little closer to them. And then he held out a couple in his hand, while he held the asshole on the ground. She leaned forward delicately, and his heart damn-near broke when she nibbled the treat off his palm. He smiled, feeling something inside swell with sheer joy. Trust was something earned, and it was hard to come by, but when you got it? Man, oh man, it was a dream come true.

She stepped a little bit closer, and he continued to offer a couple more treats, hoping that the supply in his pocket didn't run out anytime soon. He'd left the leash and the collar in his truck. Groaning and hating to, he pulled out his phone and contacted the same damn detective. When Amos answered, Kurt explained, "So I don't know what you want me to do with this guy, but he was trying to shoot my War Dog."

"And you killed him?" the detective asked with a snarl.

"No, he's here unconscious," he said. "He's the one mentoring your gang members."

"You got Slippery Simon?" His voice rose in shock.

"I don't know," Kurt said. "I'll send you a pic." He ended the call and rolled over the gunman. Even that act caused Sabine to growl. Kurt looked over at her. "He's still out cold. It's okay, sweetie." He quickly took a pic, rolled the asshole back over again, and sent it to Amos.

The cop called him a few minutes later. "Don't move," he said. "I'm on my way."

"Is it him?"

"Yeah, that's Slippery Simon. We've been after him for a long time."

"Well, you better get here fast," Kurt said and hung up.

He sat down on the guy's back, as close as he could to Sabine. "It's been a tough go, hasn't it, baby?"

She whimpered a little bit and snuggled a bit closer. He desperately wanted to reach out and touch her. She wanted that connection, that human contact too. But she was so afraid, and so was he because he didn't want to break that tenuous bond. He didn't want to break that little bit of trust growing between them.

She was too special to lose into this chaos again, but what the hell would he do with her now that the detective was coming? The last thing Kurt wanted was for her to attack the detective, although Kurt certainly understood the sentiment. He needed to make sure that she was safe when Amos appeared. Because, sure enough, the cops would be here soon and then what?

"I don't suppose you'd come with me, would you?" he whispered. He didn't have anything on him that he could use to wrap around her neck as a leash. Everything was in the truck. Yet he couldn't leave asshole here unattended. Kurt would have to wait until the detective came and went before Kurt could deal with Sabine. Just then he heard sirens in the distance. She backed up, staring in fear in the direction of the noise.

"It's all right. I'll be here when they're gone," he said. "Go hide."

Something about the term *hide* had Sabine swinging her head hard to him, and then she disappeared into the trees and melted into the background, but he could feel her gaze staring out the entire time.

Sabine was something special, but also her training was something damn creepy. She was very good at what she did. He wondered if he could keep her working, just in the civilian sector now, because she obviously had spent so much time and energy in her military career that it seemed a waste to not use it now. He didn't know if any work was around for somebody like him and her. He also didn't know if he had any right to even keep her. She wasn't free to be donated to somebody like him. But then what did he know? He'd gotten further than he had expected because he found her, after all these weeks where she had been lost.

At that thought, he sent Badger a message and a photo of the Slippery Simon dude. When that was done, Kurt heard the cops calling out. He yelled back, and they headed in his direction. He kept talking to them so they could find his location. When they neared the clearing and saw him sitting there, still atop Slippery Simon, the detective walked over and asked, "What the hell is with the gun?" He pointed to the weapon on the ground, not far from the unconscious man.

"It's not mine. It's his," Kurt said.

"And you just left it there?"

"Why not? Just the two of us were out here," he said. "I don't really care to use one, and I certainly didn't need it."

"So how does that work?" Amos asked. "He had a gun, and he came after you, and then what?"

Kurt decided that honesty would be best here. "I was working on gaining the War Dog's trust, so that I could get her under my control. I have spent a lot of time today with her back and forth. When this guy showed up, trying to shoot her, Simon was pissed that I had interrupted him, so he turned the gun on me, and Sabine attacked Simon." Kurt pointed to Simon's shoulder. "As a trained military dog, she attacked the shoulder of the hand holding the gun and brought Simon down."

The detective stared in surprise. "So you found her?"

"Yes," he said. "I found her, and, if you guys can get this asshole out of here, I might get her to trust me enough to get a rope on her and get her back to my place."

"But she bit him, that makes her dangerous."

"No, she attacked upon my orders," he said, "because, once again, I was under attack, and I was forced to defend myself."

"Says you."

"Yep, says me," Kurt said, taking a long slow breath. "Are you now doubting this story too?" Kurt looked over at the other cops who had arrived. He didn't recognize most of them, but he could tell from their attitude that a lot of news about Kurt had been shared between them.

The cops looked at Kurt curiously and then back at the man on the ground.

As if realizing he was making another spectacle and causing even more talk, the detective glared. "You don't have to make life difficult all the time for me," he said.

"Believe me. I've made enough trouble elsewhere too."

"You were a pain in the ass back then," he said, walking forward, as Kurt stood and rolled the guy over and added, "Why the hell should I think you're anything different now?"

"You don't want to see that I'm different," Kurt said quietly. "That's the problem. I'm obviously different. I have a very different set of friends and have earned their respect through the work I've done. It wasn't easy, but I did it. You just don't want to cut me any slack and see that I've changed."

"A leopard doesn't change its spots."

"A leopard doesn't have to," he snapped back, "because a leopard is, and always will be, a leopard. I may have been misguided and arrogant back then, but I'm certainly not that person now. The military made me a better man."

The detective looked at him, but there was no give in his clear gaze.

"Are you dealing with this guy or not?"

"Well, we'll take him to the station and see what he says."

"And here I thought this old man was the guy you were after," Kurt said in surprise, studying the detective. "Unless of course you're in in cahoots with Simon."

At that, the detective glared. "What the hell does that mean?"

"While on the phone, you talked about Slippery Simon being a guy you've been after for a long time, and yet, here you are, acting as if he may or may not be who you want and to hell with it. It might just be too much work for you to write this up."

"It is Slippery Simon," one of the other cops said. "And this is a huge collar, so we thank you."

"Don't fucking thank him," the detective said. "This asshole is probably running with him."

"I haven't been in town for the last thirteen years, but you have. So I'm not running with this local guy, Simon," he said, "but you might be, since you've been here the whole time since I was in the military. It would explain some of the lovely attitude I've been getting from you."

"I don't owe you anything," the detective said.

"No," Kurt said, "but I owe you a thanks."

Amos, the detective, stared at him in surprise. "Why is that?"

"Because somehow between us, during all those years where I was an asshole," he said, "I stayed out of jail. If I had gotten a record, I wouldn't have made it so easily into the navy. So thank you for being completely incompetent at your job back then. I managed to get out of this cycle of abuse in foster care to avoid the gangs and managed to make it into the navy, where I excelled."

The other guys looked at Kurt and then looked at the detective, who was steaming mad. "You made it into the navy? That's good for you," one of the cops said. "I heard that's not a terribly easy life."

Kurt looked toward the other cops and smiled. "It's not," he said, "but I knew I needed to get out before I ended up in a wooden box," he said. "I made it and made it pretty high up too. Put in a lot of years of service for this country until a really bad accident sidelined me," he said, "and now I'm on the other side, wondering what comes next."

"Yeah, you'll probably just slide back into the same damn habits," the detective guessed.

"I don't think so," he said. "I know what it's like to be a hero. I'm not too keen on getting back to the abused child I was."

"You were in foster care?" another cop asked.

"Yep, sure was. Taken away from my father when I was thirteen. He was a drunk, used to chain me up outside for fun," he said. "When he remembered that I was still alive, he'd go out and unchain me. By the time somebody finally gave me a fighting chance and turned him in, I hit foster care, but I already had an attitude big-time. I wouldn't be chained by anybody anymore."

"I'm surprised you went to the navy," the other cop said.

"I knew I needed something," he said in a flat voice. "I'd lost all respect for humanity. There's only one woman I ever loved, and the rest of the people, as far as I was concerned, were like my father—assholes. I had to find another way to live. Otherwise I wouldn't have," he said, looking down at the still unconscious Slippery Simon. "And then after all those years I became a Navy SEAL, and now I'm not sure what I'll do. I'm working for Titanium Corp out of Santa Fe, looking for War Dogs that slipped through the system."

"Wow," one of the cops said respectfully, "you became a Navy SEAL."

"You can't believe that bullshit," the detective scoffed. "Guys like this, they lie all the time."

"Yeah, sure some do. When they're desperate for a meal, when they're desperate for anything to make them feel good enough to get through the day," Kurt said, "but I never lied." He looked over at the cop who asked and nodded. "Yeah, I was an active Navy SEAL for twelve years, then sidelined for one year."

"Holy shit."

"It was time to change careers when I was injured," he said. "Most SEALs don't last beyond that."

"I heard it's pretty tough."

"It is, but there's also nothing quite like knowing that you've achieved the best of the best and that you've hit that pinnacle of your career. You're doing what you want to do to save the country," he said. "So I have absolutely no complaints about my life from the time I left this town."

"Weren't some US Navy SEALs involved when the governor's sister and brother were kidnapped in some godforsaken Iranian country? Those US scientists?" He nudged the others. "Remember that? The SEALs went in and rescued them."

At that, Kurt's lips twitched. "They did, indeed," he said. "I was one of them."

"Holy shit," the cop said, and he looked over the detective. "If the governor ever finds out that you're bad-mouthing and blackballing this guy," he said, "your career is over."

The detective looked at Kurt in surprise. "What are you talking about?"

Kurt stayed silent as he listened to the others relate one of the missions he'd been on. Truly, Kentucky's governor's brother and sister, both doctors and scientists, had been kidnapped and held for ransom over in Iran. Kurt had been part of the team who had gone over and rescued them. By the time his story was retold, Kurt could see that the atmosphere around him had shifted. He had earned their respect, but the detective would be a hell of a lot longer getting there, and that was fine. Kurt didn't give a shit if the detective ever got there, as long as he left Kurt alone. He looked down at the Slippery Simon guy and again asked, "So you want this guy or no?"

"Yep, we want him," the younger guy said with a grin. "He's Slippery Simon. He's got his fingers in all kinds of shit. And he's dangerous, with a long memory."

"In other words, watch my back?"

"Yep. When he wakes up and realizes you're the one who fingered him, he'll be all over you."

"Good warning," he said. "Thanks for that." He watched and stood off to the side, as they woke up Simon and got him groggily to his feet and then marched him to one of the cruisers.

The detective never said another word to Kurt. That was fine with him too.

As soon as they were gone, he took several steps back into the bush, sat down quietly in the growing darkness, and called out to Sabine. "It's okay, girl. It's all over with."

He heard a tiny whimper.

Kurt shifted, pulled some treats from his pocket, realizing he would be in trouble soon as he was running low, and tossed a few her way. Slowly, ever-so-slowly she crept back out again. Realizing that it was just the two of them and that she was prepared to make that step toward him made him the happiest he'd been in a very long time.

He sat here, quietly earning her trust, talking to her, just helping her to adjust to the fact that somebody in her world gave a damn. And slowly, slowly she crept a little closer and then a little closer again.

As he kept talking, he pulled out his phone and put it on Silent, just so nobody would scare Sabine if and when they called. He didn't want her startled unnecessarily. And he just wanted her to be in a safe and soothing and calm environment for a change.

It took another half hour before she came much closer. He leaned down, gently feeding her little treats on his fingers. On the next one he managed to stroke the side of her face. She stilled, staring at him, and then he did it again and again, gently stroking the side of her head and then coming up onto her jaw to scratch gently. He could see her eyes were closed with the remembrance of better times and better contact with humans, and finally she crept a little bit closer.

He gently scrubbed her neck and smoothed his hand over her head and her ears. He wanted to pick her up and hug her. He could feel the tears in his eyes as she crept a bit closer and then a little bit closer. Finally she curled up into the space between his legs and dropped her head onto his thigh, and he just sat here in the darkness with her, gently stroking her from head to toe and finding a bond between the two of them that he'd never expected.

When he could, he took a photo and sent it to Badger. The response came back almost immediately.

Wow, that was fast.

"It was," he said, when he called Badger, "but now she's breaking my heart because the bond is there, and I don't want to let her go."

"Did anybody say you had to?"

"It's not like I have a house to live in or a home where she would fit in," he replied.

"Well, sounds like it's time for you to make some decisions then."

"I'm too much in flux right now," he said.

"What were your plans for the dog?"

"I was thinking I'd take her back to the motel. I've got one that allows pets," he said, "and then I would contact you."

"Well, you've done that or almost done that," he said, "so what's the next problem?"

"Who does she belong to?

"That's a good question. She's had a pretty rough few months. I'd say that, if you've got a bond with her, we could make a good case for her to stay with you."

"I would really like that," he said. "I have to find out just how dangerous she is though."

"Yeah, there's a bunch of training, some tests that should be done. That would probably be a good idea, if you think she'd stand for it."

They talked for a few minutes more, then he dialed Laurie Ann.

"Well, you're not here," she said. "I presume you're not coming for dinner."

"I've got the dog," he said.

"What do you mean, you've *got* her?" she asked, half in excitement and half in curiosity.

"I'm in the darkness with her curled up in my legs," he said. "I'm sorry. I was so focused on gaining her trust that I shut off my phone, and I never even thought about dinner."

"Dinner is minor," she said. "Saving the dog? Now that's major."

"Well, I'm hoping so. It wasn't anywhere near as easy as I thought."

"What happened after you left?"

He gave a half laugh. "You wouldn't believe it." He quickly filled her in on the details.

"Oh, my God," she said. "As soon as you've hit town, it has been nothing but chaos."

"But good chaos," he protested. "And maybe, in a way, I'm cleaning up the streets."

"Well, that would be a change," she said with a laugh.

"I'll take the dog back to the motel," he said. "I need to find some food for her and more treats because I'm pretty well out of them."

"Well, are you still on for a barbecue tomorrow?"

He hesitated and then asked, "How do you feel about me bringing her?"

"Is she dangerous?"

"I don't think so," he said, "but I really have no idea."

"Well, there's nothing like finding out," she said. "I suggest you bring her, but make sure she's on a leash, so we have some control."

"Absolutely," he said. "I'll be a whole lot longer here, getting her on a leash and getting her back to my place anyway."

"Still be careful," she warned. "You don't know what she's been through."

"No, I don't," he said, looking down at the skinny shepherd curled into his legs. "But I know that she won't get that kind of treatment anymore. Not while I'm around."

CHAPTER 8

NO SOONER HAD Laurie Ann hung up from talking to Kurt than her phone rang again, and it was Jeremy. "Can I stay here at Frank's for dinner?"

"I thought that was a given," she said with a note of humor.

"Well, I don't want to interrupt your dinner date," he said in a mocking tone.

"Not a problem," she said easily. "Kurt just called, and he's managed to locate the dog, but now he's at a delicate point where he doesn't want to leave her alone, and he has to gain her trust in order to get a leash on her."

"He found her," her son's voice rose enthusiastically. "Oh, wow, that's awesome."

"It certainly is," she said with a smile. "If he is still coming for a barbecue tomorrow, he'll try and bring the dog too."

"That'd be great," he said. "So can I stay overnight tomorrow too?"

She groaned. "Give you an inch, and you're always trying to take a mile."

"Hey, Mom. I haven't stayed over in quite a while. You know that."

"I know," she said, "Okay. Yes, for tonight. Yes, even for tomorrow night. But be home for the barbecue tomorrow."

"Will do."

He spoke in that completely casual tone of voice, as if tomorrow's barbecue and spending time with his newfound father was absolutely of no consequence. She didn't think he felt that way, but she suspected it was his way of handling the stress and the heavy emotions. Or maybe she was the one completely out to lunch. She didn't know, but she was happy with it all. She set her phone down, when her sister called. Laurie Ann groaned.

"Wow," her sister said, in that brittle tone of hers. "Normally you're happy to hear from me."

"Of course I am," she said, desperately trying to pull back her tone of voice. "I've just gotten off the phone from multiple phone calls, so it was one of those *Darn, now who else?* kind of moments."

"Ah," she said, "I figured you were still upset at me over Kurt."

"Nope, not at all," she said. "You're entitled to your opinion."

"And you'll do what you want regardless, right?"

"Well, I have to," she said. "Otherwise, it isn't my opinion or my choice, is it?"

Her sister groaned. "Does that mean you're seeing him?"

"Well, let me put it this way. He knows about Jeremy, and Jeremy knows about him."

A shocked silence was on the other end before her sister exploded. "What? You told them? Why would you do that?"

"Because I felt that was the fair thing to do," she said. "I know you don't understand, but I won't live in fear that either one of them will find out later from someone other than me and then be mad at me."

"Well, of course, they both could be mad at you," she

said. "That's how the world runs."

"It doesn't have to," she said. "Besides, they both know, and they're both coming over for barbecue tomorrow."

"Where's Jeremy now?"

Rolling her eyes, she quickly rephrased her answer. "Jeremy's staying over at Frank's house for the night."

"Ah," she said, "well, I guess that makes sense. I sure hope you know what you're doing," she said in a warning tone.

"I don't know what I'm doing from one day to the next," she said, "but I'm trying to do the best I can. A boy's life and his whole future is ahead of him, and I don't really want to keep him separated from his father if there's no reason to. Plus, there's a very decent man who didn't know he even had a child."

"He was hardly a decent man," her sister said in exasperation.

"Maybe he's also different now," she said.

"Uh-oh." Her sister went quiet for a long moment, and then she said, in a resigned voice, "There's absolutely nothing I can do or say that'll stop this from happening, is there?"

"No," she said, "there really isn't."

"In that case, I'll get off the phone and try to ignore what's going on this weekend," she said. "Just remember who was there for you a long time ago."

"I won't forget," she said with a sudden insight into maybe why her sister was so against Laurie Ann having Kurt back in her life. "You're the only one who was there for me," she said. "Believe me. I will always remember that. And I'm so damn grateful. I wouldn't be where I am without you, Sally."

"Fine!" her sister said. "I know. I know." She hesitated. "And I don't mean to keep bringing it up. I'm just worried."

"And I love you for that too," Laurie Ann said, "because I know that the fear and the worry on your part is all about what might happen, and you're worried about me. But I'm not a child anymore. I'm not a young adult. I am somebody who has a much better understanding of life."

"Maybe," she said, "but don't forget it's still pretty easy to get taken in when we really want to believe in something."

"I know," she said quietly. "But, if you gave Kurt a chance, I think you'd really like him."

"I don't know," she said. "I don't forgive the past as easily as you."

"There's nothing to forgive," she said, "except that he has to forgive me."

"What are you talking about? He's the one who left you pregnant."

"I knew before he left," she said. "I didn't tell him. He has a lot to forgive too." And, with that, she hung up on her sister.

Laurie Ann sat here for a long moment, wondering if her sister would call her back. When she didn't, Laurie Ann slowly blew out her pent-up breath and stood and walked into the kitchen to make a cup of tea. A lot of forgiveness was required on all sides. But it had to start somewhere, and she was willing to take that first step and to acknowledge all the things that she'd done wrong. She had come a long way herself, and, damn, so had Kurt. She still admired and liked him. He was somebody she could also respect and could see he had done a ton of work on himself.

It was hard not to feel that pull, particularly when she already knew how great things had been between them. He was a hell of a man. But that also didn't mean he would stay this time around, and she didn't want to end up pregnant again when he left. That wasn't in the cards. As much as she would love to have more children, she wouldn't do it alone a second time.

And neither could she call on her sister for help anymore. That was pushing things. Some people understood and were there when trouble came, but not everybody was willing to see that repeated all over again. She'd often wondered about going to a sperm bank for a second child, but she'd held back because it just hadn't been the right time, particularly when she was going through school. Now that she was better established, it might be possible to stay home with a child although the student loans were still an issue.

She could certainly forgo one of the clinics, at least temporarily. But she didn't want to go through motherhood all alone again. It had been lonely back then. It had been scary, and she really hated not having somebody to hold her, to talk to. Besides, going through that with a true partner who was just as invested in the child's health and wellness and care as she was would be something very special. She'd lost out on all that with her first pregnancy.

Her sister had been there as much as she could—physically, monetarily—but, not having had children herself and not having any interest in having children, Sally had found it very difficult emotionally to understand why Laurie Ann wanted to go through with her pregnancy. Yet Sally had accepted a pregnant unwed Laurie Ann into her home and had helped raise Jeremy. That's what counted. And Laurie Ann had to remember that.

You don't turn your back on people because they don't like your decisions. You must remember what people have done for you in the past as well. It didn't mean that Laurie Ann had to kowtow to her sister's opinion, but Laurie Ann did have to remember to have some generosity toward that mind-set because now she understood where it was coming from.

Sally was scared of losing Laurie Ann's and Jeremy's love to another: Kurt.

For the longest time, the only people in Sally's life had been Laurie Ann and Jeremy. And Sally was probably scared that their newfound relationships with Kurt—as Laurie Ann's boyfriend, as Jeremy's father—would now change the family dynamics. And no way it couldn't. But that didn't mean it had to necessarily change in a negative way.

It was also quite possible that, if Sally opened her heart, Kurt would be more than welcome to let her remain as a strong and active member of the family. At that, Laurie Ann brought herself up cold. "Good Lord, what the hell am I doing? I'm already laying the groundwork for Kurt being a permanent part of my life."

And then she realized that Kurt might become a permanent part of Jeremy's life, as his father, but that didn't automatically mean Kurt would become a permanent part of her life. Confused, disoriented, and all of a sudden a little more worried than she expected to be, she took her tea and sat on the deck. Because now memories of divorced friends surfaced. *Oh my, it's been such a nightmare. I hate when the kids are at their dad's for the weekend and came home, completely wild on sugar and hating me from all the things that he'd said about me.*

She didn't even want to think about things like that, but, now that she had gone down that pathway, she kept remembering more horrible things her divorced friends had talked about. Things that Laurie Ann hadn't had to deal with at all and now didn't want to either. She couldn't imagine Kurt trying in any way, shape, or form to push Jeremy away from her, but she did acknowledge that the two would want to spend time together—without her. And that was disconcerting to say the least. She'd always been heavily involved in Jeremy's life. She didn't know how she felt about being the one left out now. She knew it was probably necessary for the guys to build a relationship, but having to let go after all this time? ... *Ouch.*

She sat here, mulling it all over, when she heard an odd sound in the bushes to the left. She looked around the side of the house. The covered deck came out almost like an outdoor alcove. As she looked around the side, the bushes moved again. She figured it was a raccoon or possum. She had a few animal visitors like that, so sat and waited, hoping to see it.

When she heard or saw nothing further, she settled into the past again, back in her chair, wondering at how suddenly she had an evening free, two afternoons free, and how quickly her life had been flipped. When the noise came again, she smiled and peered around the corner, wondering what critter was visiting her.

And her shocked gaze landed on a man, standing half hidden in the bushes. He studied the side of her house, but, at the sound of her movements, he turned and melted backward into the shadows. She hadn't seen enough of his face to recognize who it was. She snatched up her phone, stepped back into the house, locked the glass door, then the front door, and immediately called Kurt. When he answered, she said, "Somebody is in my backyard."

"Who?" he asked immediately.

"I don't know," she said, "just a man."

"Did you see what he was doing?"

She closed her eyes, tried to focus. "He was looking up at the side of the house. I was out on the back deck," she said.

"What's up there?"

She sucked in her breath. "My bedroom," she said.

"Is there anything on the outside wall there?"

"A trellis," she said, her voice rising in horror. "A latticework trellis is there."

"I'll be there in a few minutes," he said.

"Are you sure?" She didn't know what to say about the dog.

"Don't even ask that," he said. "I need to at least come and make sure, to see just what's going on."

And, with that, he hung up, leaving her sitting midway inside, where she could see both the rear glass door and the front door. There was still the garage door, and, dammit, she was terrified enough that she immediately raced toward the garage and locked that door too. Then she sat inside the house, a bit calmer, at least not hyperventilating like she'd been on the verge of a few minutes ago.

Why had he been looking up at her bedroom, and what difference did the lattice make? Unless he was looking to climb it? At that thought, her throat choked because it was all too possible. The last thing she wanted was to contemplate somebody breaking into the house. But her mind wouldn't let it go.

Why would anyone care? And then her mind went back to the gang scenario earlier today, where the five kids had been after her. She sent the detective a text, asking if all the teens were still locked up. He sent back a negative. Three young men were released, and the one was in the hospital.

She sat here for a long moment, thinking about that. Because, if they were free, and they were still in the same ugly mind-set as before, there was a good chance that tonight they were looking to attack her again. It's a good thing Jeremy wasn't here; she didn't want him involved in any way. This could get beyond ugly, and she didn't have a clue what to do about it. She sent him a message to just make sure he was okay. Then she texted the detective. **I had a man in the backyard tonight. Worried now.**

But she didn't expect the cop to do anything. What could he do? It's not like she had an intruder in her house; she just had somebody in the backyard, and that could have meant anything.

Did you recognize him?
I didn't get a chance to see his face.
Let me know if you see him again.

She snorted at that, tossed down her phone. "Sure," she said out loud. "I'll let you know. And it'll probably be too damn late."

And, with that, she got up and paced the house. Surely she could do something to protect yourself. But what?

It's not like she had any martial arts training, and it was a horrible feeling to realize that she felt completely vulnerable to the world around her right now. She could call her sister, and then her sister would come racing over, and that would put her in danger. Which would not solve anything and she could get hurt herself. Laurie Ann's mind continued to loop in endless circles, until she heard a truck drive up. She raced to the front window and peered through the side of the curtains to see it was Kurt.

He hopped out, and, with the driver's door open, he

stood facing the inside of the truck. And slowly, as if almost painfully, a shepherd jumped down beside him. Laurie Ann gasped in shock. He got the War Dog on a leash.

She raced to the front door and opened it.

He expected her and held up a hand and said, "Don't rush, please."

She stopped and nodded. "Can I come forward?"

The shepherd looked at Laurie Ann curiously, but no aggression was in her eyes.

Kurt nodded. "That you can do," he said. "Come stand beside me."

She walked a few steps and called out, "Hello, girl."

The shepherd's tail wagged.

"She's so skinny," she said to Kurt. "How can anybody mistreat a dog?"

"I don't know that she was mistreated as much as abandoned by a society that doesn't take care of its animals or its war heroes. It's sad. She deserves better."

"I've always loved animals," she murmured.

"As you know, I have too, but it was never something that worked into my life before."

"And yet apparently that's changed," she said with a laugh.

He bent down in front of the shepherd, gently stroking the side of her head and neck. "And you've got to remember how this is all new to Sabine, so she has to decide as to whether each human being can be trusted or not."

"And you think she's at the point where she knows most aren't?" She desperately wanted to crouch down and cuddle the poor dog, but it was too early.

"From the way I've seen her today, I would assume so," he said. "But animals can be very trusting, even after the fact.

So, while she has been abused, that doesn't mean she'll remain in that same wounded-warrior mentality."

"I just want to hug her," she said, as she crouched down beside him and gently reached out a hand.

"Her name is Sabine," he said gently. He placed a hand on hers and nudged her hand closer to the shepherd, who leaned closer and sniffed fingers and then let her muzzle nudge Laurie Ann's fingertips. Delighted, Laurie Ann gently stroked the skinny dog. "We need to get her some food," she said.

"I've got a little in the truck, just not enough for very many days."

"Well, I have leftovers. Or I could order in a delivery," she said. "Or, if you want to be here with the dog, I can go collect some."

"We won't leave you alone for a while," he said quietly. "At least not until I know what's going on."

"On that note," she said, "good luck with trying to figure it out because it doesn't make sense."

"Show me where you saw the guy." She nodded and led the way around the back through the gate, the shepherd coming with them. Laurie Ann watched as the shepherd approached the back of the house with her ears up and her tail casually moving around. "She seems to be interested in everything around her," she said.

"I think so. I certainly don't know very many of the commands she has learned, so I've reached out to Badger to look for her previous trainer to see what she understands," he said. "Generally there's a set protocol for commands, but everybody has the little special things that they do with their dogs."

"I still can't believe that she ended up in this situation."

"Well, unfortunately it's what happened," he said, "so let's just try to make her next years the best they can be."

"Are you keeping her?" At his nod, they walked around the backyard, and Laurie Ann noted that he'd let the shepherd have a good six foot lead. "Do you think it's safe for her to be here?"

"Safe for her, or safe for you?" he asked with the note of humor.

She smiled. "For both, I guess," she said. "She seems very well-behaved."

"She's very well trained. She's just had a rough couple months," he said. He studied the shepherd as they walked around the right side of the property in the opposite direction of where her intruder had been.

"She seems very alert."

"She is but not too bothered. She's trying to sort out the smells in the area and just what she's looking at and looking for. She doesn't know me. She doesn't know you. She doesn't know this area," he said. "But she's still working to sort it all out in her head."

"Did you have any trouble getting a collar and leash on her?" she asked.

"No," he said. "By the time I stood up where she was cuddling with me, she followed me to the truck on her own. As soon as I put a collar and the leash on her, she jumped up beside me in the truck."

"So she really wanted to come with you."

"I think she was damn grateful to have a decent human in her life," he said with a quiet smile down at the dog. As they got around to the far left side, immediately the dog growled in the back of her throat, and her ears went back ever-so-slightly, and her lip curled.

"Okay, that's not a good sign," she said, taking a step back.

"Well, it's a good sign," he said, "if you think about it. This is where your intruder was, wasn't he?"

She looked around and then nodded. "Yes. How does Sabine know that?"

"Her training. But whether it's because she recognizes him as her recent enemy or as somebody who was here for no good, that's hard to say."

"And how would she know that?"

"Well, if it was her own enemy," he said, "it would be one of the people who probably have been giving her a hard time and possibly tried to hurt her. However, if it was somebody trying to hide here on your property, Sabine's been trained to sniff out the enemy hiding in various scenarios. So that's just part of her training."

"Wow," she said, "they really use dogs for that?"

"Yes, they really do. The problem came when the enemy shot the dogs, which told our men where the enemy was, but often the dogs would hide to avoid getting shot."

"But often the War Dogs were shot?"

"There are always casualties in war, whether canine or human. Of course canine deaths were preferred over human."

She knew that logically, but it still bothered her.

"It bothers all of us," he said quietly, reading her mind. "No animal lover wants to see them suffer."

"Especially now. She's been through enough."

"She has, indeed. That's why we're doing what we're doing—to keep her safe now."

The dog sniffed out the area thoroughly. As she watched, Laurie Ann asked, "Can you track with her? Can she track the intruder?"

"Maybe." He sat down beside Sabine on the grass and let her just sniff the whole area. Then she whined and ran around the house, heading toward the front gate.

"Does this go where I think it does?" Kurt asked.

"Back to the road that leads to the front of the property," she said.

He nodded, opened it up, and let the dog through. Immediately she bounced through, pulling at the leash. He came along behind Sabine, with Laurie Ann following up in the rear. She closed the gate behind her and watched as Kurt and the dog raced to the edge of the road. There Sabine stopped. She milled around in the same place, whined, and then sat down and barked.

Laurie Ann walked over to him. "What does that mean?"

"It means that your stranger most likely got into a vehicle and left that way."

"Well, the good news is," she said, "he's likely left. The bad news is, we don't know why he was here in the first place."

"And who brought him here, if he didn't come alone?"

"None of that appeals in any way," she said.

He nodded. "Let's go back into the backyard," he said.

She led the way because she was nearest. She opened the gate and held it for them to pass. As soon as they got into the backyard, he turned and headed toward the wall of the house, where the stranger had been staring up at.

"Interesting," Kurt said.

"And again that doesn't sound very positive," she said, staring up at the same place he was focused on and seeing nothing. "What is it you're seeing?"

"Well, if it was me," he said, "I'd be analyzing how to

get into your house, and that trellis offers a way."

"And that's what I was afraid you would say," she said flatly.

"We don't know for sure that that's what he was up to, you know?" he said.

"No, but what else would it be?"

"Unfortunately I don't see another answer that's quite as good," he said. "But that doesn't necessarily mean it's a bad thing. He knew he was seen, and he's taken off."

"But, if he was coming back anyway, he would now know what he needed to get inside," she said.

And he nodded. "Exactly. Do you sleep up there?"

"I do. Right now Jeremy is over at his friend's for the night," she said, "which is a good thing. But now I don't want him to come back and to be in danger at all."

"That, of course, begs another question. Was it you they were after? The house they were after? Or Jeremy?" He stepped back several feet and looked up. "The lattice itself won't hold him though," he said, "but it'd be pretty easy to jump up onto that deck up there."

She stared up at the distance and shook her head in disbelief. "Did you say, *pretty easy?*"

He nodded. "Absolutely."

"That's not what I want to hear. You know that, right?"

He nodded. "Most people don't think about it. They think, since they're on the second floor, they're safe, and it's not true. What happens is, you become pinned up there because you don't know how to get out yourself, and jumping down will often cause a broken leg or other injury," he murmured.

He grabbed the trellis and pulled hard. It stayed put. He frowned. "I really don't like that. Do you know if he touched it?"

"I don't know," she said. "I was just sitting out here, having tea, when I heard him in the first place."

"He never said anything to you?"

"No," she said, shivering with the remembrance. "I'm glad he didn't," she said. "Otherwise I'd be hearing his voice in my nightmares."

He nodded quietly. "Unfortunately it looks like you'll be in this mess until it is over with anyway."

"And how do we get it over with?" she asked.

"Well, we have to find out why he's here and stop him from coming back, and that means capturing him. Would you recognize him?"

She frowned and thought about it. "I don't think so," she said slowly. "I didn't see his face, but I saw his general build. But I don't really know."

"So you didn't see him clearly, but, given the right light and the right angle, you might find a hint of recognition or something like that?"

"Something like that, yes," she said, "but it's not like I could sit down with an artist and tell you what he looked like."

"Right," he said with a smile. He stepped back, looking at all the walls of the house, and they kept walking all the way around until they were back at the front door. The whole time he was studying the layout of the house. "You haven't lived here very long?"

"No," she said, "it's been about nine months."

"Before that?"

"I rented a condo," she said. "I finally scraped enough to pull together for this place. And it was close to Frank's home, so Jeremy was, of course, delighted."

"They're best friends, huh?"

"Yeah," she said with a gentle smile.

"And Frank's a good kid?"

"The best. His dad's another doctor," she said. "Not that that makes him above reproach, but I do know him, as I've worked with him several times."

"Sometimes that's all you can hope for," he said. "Kids have to grow up making their own choices."

"And even when they're growing up, they have to make their own choices," she said. "My sister still doesn't believe that."

"Your sister sees you as somebody who was taken advantage of, that she had to help out in a bad situation, and, if you make your own decisions now, maybe you'll make ones that don't include her," he said gently.

"I was thinking of that earlier today. She's very unhappy that you're back in town."

"Of course she is. She's expecting me to leave you pregnant again and take off."

"I don't think it's quite that simple," she said.

"You can't blame her either."

"No," she said, "but it's also like my family doesn't see that I've grown up, and that's a little hard to accept."

He chuckled. "I wonder if we ever grow up to the rest of our family. I think they always see us as children."

"I hope not," she said. "I'd like to think that I can see Jeremy growing up."

"He's in an interesting stage of life right now," he said. "Thirteen." He shook his head. "Man, that takes me way back."

"And probably not in a good way," she said.

"It wasn't all bad," he said. "It was pretty tough toward

the end though."

"I'm sorry your childhood was much less than ideal."

"Everybody's childhood is much less than ideal," he said, "but it's a card you're dealt. You play the game the best you can. You hope you get a chance to fix things, if you screw up. In my case I did, and I'm forever grateful for that."

"Good," she said. "Now what do we do about this guy?"

"I think we should set a trap for him," he said without hesitation.

She looked at him in shock. "What?"

"Well, think about it," he said. "We don't want him to come back, but, if he does, I suggest we make sure that we capture him at the same time."

"And how will you do that?"

"Well, if it was me breaking in, I would still try this trellis," he said, "but I would probably use a rope or a hook to throw up and grab the balcony. So we want to trigger that balcony door up there to make sure that, if he does get that far, we can trap him, so he doesn't get away again."

"Well, that sounds great," she said, "as long as you're sticking around to capture him. I really don't want to be the one with a caught intruder in the house."

"Oh, that's not happening," he said. "I'm not leaving until we know we've got him."

She felt a bright sense of relief and, at the same time, a shiver of excitement. She avoided the one question that she really wanted to ask, which was, *Where was he planning on sleeping?* Because, Jesus, they were just rekindling their friendship and were so far away from that level of intimacy. Yet she couldn't believe that her hormones were ready to drag him into her bed. "Does that mean you are moving in? And what about Sabine here?" she asked, looking down at the dog.

"Sure, certainly will," he said. "And, yes, Sabine too. She'll be the biggest and earliest alarm we've got."

"But we don't know her yet or trust her."

"Nope, but I trust her instincts, and I trust that she's already had enough abuse from a lot of assholes," he said. "She'll be doing what she can to keep us safe, if only for her own sake."

"I guess that's a priority in her world now too, isn't it? If you're safe, then she's safe."

"Something like that," he said with a smile.

"Well, that's great," she said. "You want to go inside? I'll put on some tea or coffee."

"A cup of coffee would be great, but, if it's too late for you, I'm happy with tea too."

She smiled. "Remember how we used to make tea from the herbs we found on the side of the road?"

"Yeah, I was into the prepper thing back then too at one time, wasn't I?"

"You were," she said. "You were adorable."

He snorted at that. "I was one messed-up kid. I don't even know how you saw something to like."

"I found lots to like," she said. "Maybe it's because I understood you better than you understood yourself."

"Maybe," he said. "I still don't quite see what you ever saw in me."

"All the girls were after you," she said in the teasing voice. "It wasn't just me."

"Yeah, they were." He sent her that lopsided grin. "That was kind of cool."

She laughed out loud. "Everybody loves to be a heart-throb."

"Didn't matter to me so much," he said. "You're the one I wanted to be with."

"I know," she said. "We were both obviously young and naive. At least I was," she said, rolling her eyes.

He chuckled and said, "Yet look at the job you did," he said. "Jeremy's fantastic."

"He is," she said with a big smile. "Of all the things that I feel good about in my life, he's the big one," she said with a bright smile. "No regrets in having him at all."

As they headed back into the kitchen, he left the porch door open and slowly dropped Sabine's leash.

"Is that safe?" Laurie Ann asked from the kitchen, as she measured the coffee.

"Let's find out."

At that, the dog immediately walked to the doorway's edge, as Kurt stopped and watched. Then Sabine walked the perimeter of the fenced yard and came back again, where she sat down in front of the open door.

"I guess she's not used to being inside, is she?" Laurie Ann asked in sudden understanding. "That's why you left the door open."

"I don't want her to feel pent up or captured," he said. "She needs to know that she's been rescued and lifted up out of her ugly life. I know it seems like it's a minor difference, but it's one that matters."

"All of it matters," she said quietly. "I certainly understand the need not to feel caged."

"Right," he said, "that's how you felt when you found out you were pregnant."

"I did," she said, staring at him. "How did you know?"

"Because that's how I felt when I was here in this town," he said. "I needed desperately to get out. I didn't know why.

I didn't know how. I just knew I needed to leave."

"And, in my case, I knew I needed to have Jeremy. I just didn't know how or why or what it would entail," she said. "The hardest part was my parents."

"I understand," he said. "And I have to deal with the fact that I wasn't there for you all these years. It's easy to say, *I didn't know*, but, at the same time, neither did I check. So I have to live with that too."

"Well, why don't we just start fresh?" she said. "I'm totally okay to do that."

"That sounds like a deal," he said. "You're very forgiving."

"I'm still me," she said. "Whether you remember all the nuances of the life that we shared back then, I was always a very forgiving person."

"I do remember," he said. "You're also very loving, very loyal, and extremely defensive of me."

"Well, an awful lot of people out there wanted to bash you. The more they did, the more I went against them," she said, chuckling. "If only they knew that."

"Your parents would have had a heart attack if they understood that," he said with a grin.

"So it's a good thing they didn't," she said, "because Jeremy is still well worth having."

"I agree," he said. He looked around and said, "And I know you said there were leftovers, but, if there aren't enough, I'm quite happy to order in."

"What would you order?" she asked curiously.

He frowned and thought about it and said, "Well, I would probably order in burgers and a few spare patties for the dog."

"Right," she said, looking over at the opened door,

where the shepherd lay. "She hasn't eaten, has she?"

"Not a whole lot, no," he said, "just the treats."

"Well, we have to fix that." She went to the fridge, opened it up, and said, "I've got leftover roast beef."

"Do you have any bread?"

"Yes, of course." She looked over and asked, "Why?"

He said, "I'll have a roast beef sandwich, and, if there's enough for the dog, I'll split it with her, depending on how much there is. How about you?"

"I'm not sure I can eat yet. My emotions have my stomach stirred up. But I may eat something later." She pulled out a good-sized slab of roast beef, and he nodded.

"Was this designated for another meal?"

"No," she said, "not at all."

"Since you've got bread, I'll make it." When she brought out a loaf of French bread, he nodded with a big smile. "And that's perfect," he said. He quickly cut several slabs and then sliced the roast beef paper-thin.

"Are you just having an open-faced sandwich, like that?" she asked.

"Yep, I sure am," he said. "I love it this way."

She smiled and watched as he very capably cut up the bread and the food, and then she asked, "What about Sabine?"

"Do you have a couple bowls or plates for her?"

"Yep." She got down two large wide bowls.

He immediately chopped up some roast beef and put it in one.

"She shouldn't have just straight meat, should she?"

"You had any leftover rice, some carrots, some cooked veggies?"

She brought out more leftovers and then watched as he

put a bunch together, mashed them up, added a little bit of butter, and put that all in the other bowl. He set that down first for the dog. The dog looked at him, not too impressed, but she hadn't eaten very much lately, so she dug in. When she'd eaten half of it, he dropped the roast beef in on top of the rest. She immediately devoured the rest of the bowl.

"Wow," she said, "that was pretty tricky."

"Well, Sabine's smart, and it won't work all the time," he said. "But she's so hungry and tired, and she's done without enough that, right now, she's quite happy to eat whatever we give her."

"We have to put dog food on the grocery list," she said.

"I know. I'm just not sure I want to take her out too much to many public places yet," he murmured. He reached over and gently stroked the shepherd. She took a few steps to come closer and leaned against his leg.

"I love to see that," she murmured. "Already a bond has formed between the two of you. Have you considered the implications of that?"

"I haven't stopped thinking about it," he said. "Can't let her go now."

"So you can keep her?"

"I think so," he said. "I've talked to my bosses about it."

"I don't know where you live," she said and then shook her head. "I haven't even asked you about any of that, but can you have a dog?"

"I've been living in New Mexico in a rented apartment temporarily, while I decide on my new future. As to keeping her, I've been trying to figure out where I'm going with my life."

"Did you figure it out?" she asked with a smirk. "Because, if you did, maybe you could help me figure mine out."

"You know exactly where you're going," he said, looking at her. "You've got a beautiful son. You've got a beautiful home, and you have the career you've always wanted."

"I do," she said with a smile. "But somehow it still feels a little on the empty side."

"That's because I'm not in it," he said with a bright grand smile.

She laughed. "Unfortunately you could be right."

KURT SAT DOWN with his roast beef sandwich. The dog sat at his side and watched him hungrily.

"Could she still be hungry?" Laurie Ann asked. She hopped up and brought over a bowl of water. The dog barely looked at it.

He smiled and nodded. "After so long without food, she'll probably overeat for quite a while, until she figures out that there'll be a continuation of food in her world."

"I can't imagine what she went through," she murmured.

He took another bite. Once he swallowed, he said, "And that's what makes you so special too."

She shook her head. "Doesn't feel like it," she said, sitting down beside him. She sighed, looked over at him, and said, "Any thoughts about moving here permanently?"

"Well, there weren't before I came," he admitted, "but now I can't think of anything else. I gather you don't want to leave this area?" he asked.

"I'd just as soon not," she said. "It's taken me a long time to build up the business, to get the jobs at the clinics that I have," she said, "to have patients who count on me, but I can also see that you have a problem with your history here."

"Yes, but we don't have to let that stop us from having a life here."

She looked at him with a gentle smile. "It seems like it stopped us a lot over the years."

"No longer," he said. "The thing is, just like back then, I'm still not a good prospect."

She stared at him in astonishment. "What do you mean?"

"Your family will be quick to point out that I don't have a real job. Don't have any job as far as they're concerned. No way to support you or to look after you."

She shook her head. "You'll fix that," she said firmly.

He burst out laughing. "Maybe," he said, "but that does not mean that I have an answer right away."

"Maybe not," she said, "but you currently are working, even if it's unpaid, which I understand is more of a volunteer position."

He nodded.

"And I appreciate the fact that you're doing that because of the War Dog," she said, looking down Sabine. "So that's not a negative in my book."

"Not in your book maybe, but in a lot of people's books," he said. "Although I have a few ideas about what I want to do with my life, but I haven't exactly locked anything down. Plus, your family will also consider me a washout because I got injured. So they'll be afraid that you'll spend your life looking after an injured man who is incapable of supporting himself."

"Which would all be lies," she said. "You're not the kind to sit on the couch and play video games, while your wife works."

He didn't say a word about the *wife* part, but she was right. He wasn't, but her trust in him was touching. Misguided, because she didn't really know who he was anymore, but still very touching. "They'll still scream."

"They can scream as loud and as hard as they want," she said. "I don't have anything to do with my parents anymore. And I gave up trying to please them a long time ago."

"Good," he said, "but, for the purposes of keeping peace in the family, you know very well how hard it is to go against all that."

"I am only close to my sister, and as long as I keep her in my life, I think you're right. I'm sure she'll come around."

"If I had a good job," he said with a smile, "then I'm sure she'd be easier to come around."

"It's sad, isn't it?" she said.

"No, it's called love. She worries about you. You've been in a tough spot before, and she doesn't want to see you in that same spot again."

"I know," she said, "and I love her for it. At the same time, it's frustrating."

"That's family for you," he said, chuckling.

She smiled and nodded. "Have you thought about what you want to do?"

"Like I said, I have a few ideas," he said easily. "But I don't have anything locked down because I was thinking about what I would do in Santa Fe."

She winced at that. "I guess I hadn't considered that. If you move here, you have to start all over again, don't you?"

"Which, in a way, is the right time to do this then because I'm basically starting all over again anyway."

She nodded and smiled. "So any time you get any ideas

about what you want to do, I'd love to hear them."

"When I figure it out, I'll let you'll know," he said, keeping a close counsel, because he really didn't have a clue. Not here. Not now. He knew the detective had pissed him right off, and that would be a bit of an issue, but he didn't know if law enforcement was something he wanted to do and whether he could even do it physically.

"What about working with the dog?" she asked, looking down at Sabine.

"Maybe. I don't have the same training that her handlers had," he said, "but it doesn't mean that I can't get it."

"Oh, I never even thought of that. I guess you do have resources, benefits, don't you?"

He smiled and nodded and said, "I have a lot of resources. If I want to go back to school, I can. If I want to get extra training, I can."

She brightened at that. "That's a huge gift then."

"It is, as long as you know what you want to do," he said in a droll tone. As he picked up the last piece of his sandwich, Sabine barked. He looked down at her, raised an eyebrow, and asked, "Was that a question, or was that a request?"

She barked one more time, and her tail started to wag. He took the roast beef off the bread and held it out to her. Totally ignoring the ketchup, she wolfed it down and then dropped her chin on his knee, while he popped the bread into his mouth. He reached down and gently scratched her.

"She's already such a character," Laurie Ann said in wonder.

"That she is," he said with a bright smile. "We just have to see what kind of character she'll end up being."

"But you'll keep her regardless, won't you?"

"Yeah," he said, "I will."

She beamed. "Good."

"Well, that answers that question," he said. "I was afraid to ask how you felt about it."

"Well, of course, we want to keep her," she said. "How could you possibly let her go now?"

He looked at Laurie Ann, wondering how he'd ever thought that leaving her was a good idea. He shook his head. "I do get upset when I think about all the time we've wasted," he murmured. "I don't even know how we're back here again—as if all the years, the goodbyes never happened."

"Don't think about it," she said. "That's the path for disaster."

"Well, I can agree with that," he said. "I just don't want to miss any more."

She held out her hand. He laced his fingers through hers and squeezed tight. "I guess something about living and dying makes you really question life, doesn't it?"

"When I lay in the hospital bed, and I was all alone," he said, "I did wonder for a long time if anybody in this world would give a damn if I was no longer on the planet. It's very sobering to come to that realization that there really wasn't anyone. Sure, I had teammates and people I'd helped in the world, and they would have given a thought and maybe been sad and sorrowful for a few minutes, and that would have been it," he said. He could feel some of that pain still inside. "When you realize that nobody really loves you, that you really have nobody to love, and that nobody cares one way or the other if you're here," he said, "it sure makes you take another look at life."

"And it's given you another chance at life," she murmured.

He smiled. "So true. And I'm determined to make the best of it."

"Sounds good to me, but we have to get rid of this asshole who's trying to crawl into my house. So we can see what we have between us."

"Speaking of which," he said, "I want to take a cup of coffee upstairs and peruse where he would come inside and what we can do about that."

She immediately hopped up and poured two cups of coffee, and, as he stood, the dog immediately bounced to her feet, her gaze watchful.

"So, is she watching you to see if you'll leave her," Laurie Ann asked, "or is she watching to see what we're doing?"

"In this instance," he said, "both. She's been left before. I think she'll probably have abandonment issues for quite a while, until she learns that she's secure and healthy and happy and that life will be good again."

"Well, let's hope she gets there fast," she murmured.

"Yep, I hear you." As they walked up the stairs, she led the way and said, "The master's right here, and this leads into the master bathroom but also to the closet."

He stepped in behind her, noted the large space, and said, "This is a decent-size room."

"Isn't it? It's one of the reasons I loved it," she said. "All the time I was living with my sister, Jeremy and I had two very small rooms and a bath, and it really got to me after a while," she said, "so it was one of the advantages of this master."

"I like it." He walked over to the deck door and pulled open the slider. "At least this makes enough noise that you would think it would wake you in the night."

"I'm a heavy sleeper," she confessed, "and often I don't even hear my alarm in the morning."

"In other words, he might have made it inside without you knowing."

"I'm afraid so." And she really was worried about that.

He could see it on her face. "Well, it's a good thing that I'll be here tonight."

She said, "Yeah, and then what about tomorrow night?"

He looked over, grinned, and said, "How do you feel about a permanent house guest?"

She snorted. "I don't think we're quite there yet."

"Nope, but," he said, "nobody's coming after you while I'm around," he said, "so we need to come to some arrangement. What other rooms do you have here?"

CHAPTER 9

Laurie Ann led the way and showed him Jeremy's bedroom, which was another large room, with his big gaming setup, his messy bed, his dirty clothes on the floor, his sports team posters and a big hockey jersey all on the wall.

And Kurt smiled. "Typical boy's room."

"Well, I'm grateful it's not pinup poster girls," she said with an eye roll.

He laughed out loud. "At that age I wouldn't be at all surprised."

"Neither would I," she said, "so I'll be grateful for what we have." She laughed. At that, she walked over to the spare room, which was on the other side of the house and faced the street.

He looked it over and said, "I know you don't want to hear this, but any chance you want to sleep in here tonight and let me stay in the master?" he asked. "At least that way, if the guy comes back, he'll find me, not you."

She hated to put him in danger like that. "I don't want you to get into trouble because this asshole's after me."

"I'd love to get into trouble because this asshole's coming for you," he said gently. "I live for guys like this."

She frowned at him. "You always were like that," she said, "you and that badass attitude."

"Well, now I have the skills," he said with a small smile, "to go with it."

"Are you sure?" she said. "I don't want you hurt, and you're already injured." At that, he shook his head, and she could see she'd insulted him. "Or you're not that badly injured, are you?"

He lifted his pant leg and showed her his prosthetic.

She stared in surprise. "I didn't know," she said. "I had no idea."

"Good," he said, "the last thing I want is for you to see me as handicapped."

"I can't imagine a less handicapped person in my life," she retorted. "But I still don't want you setting yourself up as a victim here."

"Hardly a victim," he said with a smile. "A willing target. And then, when he comes inside, he'll have to deal with me."

"If you're sure," she said doubtfully.

"I'm very sure," he said. "It's still early yet tonight, but let's get whatever you need for the night moved over." She grabbed her big down comforter, and he smiled and said, "I'm not planning on sleeping on the bed," he said. "I'll sleep on the floor."

"That doesn't make any sense," she said. "You might as well sleep in my bed."

"I'm not sure I'm ready for that," he said with an odd note.

She looked at him and asked, "In what way?"

"I'll want so much more," he said, "and sleeping with all those smells and scents will be that much harder."

She flushed, realizing exactly how much passion still simmered underneath the surface for him too. "We always were good that way, weren't we?" she said with a half smile.

"We were deadly," he said. "I've never met another woman who made me lose control quite like you."

"Ha! And I didn't even know that's what I was doing," she said with a big grin.

He burst out laughing. "That's another thing," he said, walking over and taking her in his arms, where he could just hold her. "We always laughed. I remember that very distinctly."

"Yep," she said, "we always could see the bright side, and we always could laugh at each other and at the world," she said. "It's a sad day if we ever lose that."

"Sometimes it's a sad world," he said.

She leaned back and looked up at him. "Absolutely. Now let me go make up the bed in the other room for me," she said. "Then we'll see what we can make up for you here."

He stepped back, and she quickly carried the bedding and her nightie into her spare room.

She could use the second bathroom just fine, even though she preferred her own en suite, but it wasn't like this would be a forever scenario. And, if it made life easier and made him feel better, then fine, although she really didn't want to see him hurt. Now that she knew he was missing a leg, it was that much worse. And she knew immediately that he would hate that she thought that way.

She groaned, hoping it was low enough, but he heard it.

He turned, looked at her, and said, "What?"

She decided that honesty was the best answer, and she said, "I was thinking it wasn't fair because you're already injured with a prosthetic, and you shouldn't be doing this, and then I realized how angry you would be if you thought I was thinking that way."

"And I will be," he said, "if you continue to think that

way." He studied her intently. "I am no less the warrior than I was," he said, "and I damn well will not tolerate anybody thinking that."

His voice had that clipped edge that told her how very desperately unhappy he was to hear her voice that. "But I still needed to say it," she said gently. "Anything else would have been a lie."

At that, he burst out laughing. "And I remember that too," he said. "You could send me from fury to laughter in a heartbeat."

"I never quite understood why you were so volatile," she said in a musing voice, "but you were. You'd be up, and then you'd be down."

"And that was all you," he said. "You'd send me into this fury, by saying something completely insulting, and then it would be so obvious that you hadn't meant it as an insult in any way, and I'd break up laughing." He shook his head. "I don't know if it was the naiveté or if we were just so very different, but it seemed like everything about you was so fresh and young and different."

"That would have worn off quickly," she said with a smile.

"Maybe," he said, "but it sure hasn't worn off over all these years."

She looked up at him, shadows in her eyes, and she said, "And what if it's not for real?"

"Well," he said, "I guess we have to take the walk together and see. Because otherwise anything less will seem like I missed out on something very major all over again," he said, "and I couldn't live with that."

She smiled and felt tears in the back of her eyes. "You used to say the damnedest things," she said, "and this is just the same thing all over again."

"But I meant them then, and I mean them now," he said. "You were always very precious to me. I don't know why I needed to get out of town, but obviously I understood more than I thought I would about just how bad and how much I needed to grow up and how I couldn't do that here."

"And it never occurred to me," she said, "how long the memories of the people here were." She added, "If I thought moving my job and my son was an easy thing, I'd consider moving, just so you could have a fresh start somewhere else."

"It's okay," he said, "because I've been through enough places and done enough good works in the world that I can stand tall and proud. I know I made a lot of mistakes back then, but," he added, "they weren't all fatal, and I recovered from most of them."

"And the detective?"

"Screw him," he said with a casual air. "If I worried about every asshole out there in the world, I'd do nothing but fight, and I gave that up a long time ago."

She smiled. "Once again you have all the answers," she said, shaking her head. "And that was something I couldn't believe either. While I dillydallied and didn't know what to do and how to do it, you'd already made decisions and were ahead of me in no time."

"I was never hampered by a lack of decision-making," he said. "I was hampered by jumping in too quick and not thinking things through. You used to think things through, and, when you were done, you would come back with a decision. By then I was already ten steps down the path, but it didn't mean they were the right ten steps or that they were even on the right path," he said with a sideways grin.

She walked into the guest bathroom and then looked

down at her watch. "Oh my," she said. "And here I was ready to brush my teeth, so I could turn around and go to bed, but it's still early yet."

"It doesn't feel very early," he admitted. He checked his watch. "It's nine-thirty. When do you normally go to bed?"

She shrugged. "About ten-thirty normally."

"And now?"

"I'm tired," she said. "I wouldn't mind going to bed soon, but it doesn't have be right now."

"I'll do a walk around the property anyway," he said. "So go ahead and get ready for bed, and I'll take Sabine for another visit outside, and, when we come back in, it's probably better if we just go to sleep."

"Is that because you're not expecting to get much sleep?" she asked shrewdly. "Or some other reason?"

"Lots of reasons," he said, "but your guess is as good as any. I just don't want to end up in a situation where we're both exhausted tomorrow when dealing with Jeremy."

"Ouch," she said, thinking about her son and Kurt. "I'm really hoping that goes well."

"Maybe," he said. "I'm obviously hoping it will too, but I also know that just because it might go well tomorrow doesn't mean there isn't work to be done."

"I know," she said sadly. "You're right."

As she watched, he got up, called Sabine to him, and the two walked back downstairs. She didn't know how long he would be gone, but she took advantage and quickly went through her nightly ritual and then realized she wanted a shower anyway. She hopped in, had a quick shower, and, by the time she came out, she heard them downstairs, rummaging in the kitchen. She wondered if they were looking for more food. Anything was possible. She dressed, and, with her wet towel hung up on the hook on the side, she stepped out and called down to him and said, "I'm out of the shower, if you want one."

"That's a good idea," he said, coming upstairs. "I've locked up downstairs, and I didn't see anything outside."

She smiled with relief. "You know what? My stranger could have had nothing to do with us," she said. "It could have been a complete accident. Maybe he was looking for a completely different house."

"Maybe," he said.

She smiled, reached up, kissed him gently on the cheek, and said, "Have a good night." And she walked into the spare room and closed the door.

HE DESERVED A medal for this, dammit. Kurt stared at the door to the room that he so badly wanted to join her in and then turned and forcibly walked toward the master. He didn't want to chase her out of her usual bedroom, but, given the circumstances, this was the most sensible way to do things. And he wasn't planning on sleeping in her bed because he knew he'd never sleep. The memories would crush him. After he'd washed up, he pulled a set of blankets from the closet and stretched them out on the floor and laid down. Sabine came over, and he had laid down a blanket just for her and patted it. She immediately curled up at his side and cuddled in close. He wrapped his arm around her and whispered, "Just for tonight, girl." She whimpered a little bit, and he gently stroked her until she fell asleep.

He lay here, quietly thinking about all the things he could do with his life, realizing it was definitely time for some decision-making. He hadn't expected to be here or to even want to stay here in town, but the decision had been made for him. As he lay here, his phone buzzed. *Badger.* Kurt went through his messages and then ended up calling him. "The shepherd's beside me," he said. "I sent you a picture."

"I know. I just saw it. Looks like she's in decent hands."

"I don't want to give her up," he said.

"You don't have to," Badger said. "I've cleared it with the commander."

That was terrific news. He hugged Sabine gently. "Good," he said.

"And of course the commander wants to know that you're capable of keeping the dog in good health and shape."

"Meaning, do I have a job and all that other good stuff."

Badger laughed. "Something like that."

"Doing a lot of thinking about that right now," he said, "considering where I'm at."

"And how's your son?"

"Well, I've met him. He's the spitting image of me, that's for sure. He's a big strapping kid, and he's just thirteen," he said. "I still find it hard to believe."

"Well, you've only had a couple days to digest that new info. Even now that Kat's pregnant," he said, "it's taking us quite a bit of adjustment time. So you've got an almost-adult ready-made son, and it'll take time too."

"We'll have a barbecue tomorrow, as a family," he said, "but I'm staying at her house tonight in her bedroom on the floor," he said for clarity, "because she had an intruder in the backyard today."

"What?" Badger's voice sharpened. "Is it connected to what's going on with the dog or with you?"

"Well, the gang certainly gave her a hard time, and I

stepped in. Of course then we had the older guy, trying to shoot Sabine," he said. "The local detective from my youth still has it in for me. So we've made some enemies in a very short time frame."

"You can always judge a man by his enemies."

"Well, we got a bunch of them on our ass right here, right now, so, whatever it means, this latest guy wasn't here for tea and cookies."

"They never are," Badger said. "What do you need?"

"Well, I'd love a weapon, but I don't have one, so I'll make do without," he said. "Did I mention that the detective here is still a pain in the ass?"

"Yep. I've already made a few phone calls about him. You should be getting a couple phone calls about it."

"In what way?"

"Well, one was a discussion about a job," Badger said. "I said I wasn't sure where you would end up and what you were up to or what thoughts you had about a new career."

"What kind of a job?"

"A watchdog for the cops."

"Something like internal affairs?" he said, frowning.

"Not quite. You wouldn't be doing the investigations into their behavior, but you would be keeping the reports and going over them, how they've acted, depending on various circumstances. More like pointing out where they could improve."

"Well, the detective certainly wouldn't like that," Kurt said with a laugh.

"I don't know if I'd like it either. But it's a good-paying job, and it would be something that you're uniquely qualified for," he said. "They would like to talk to you."

"Interesting," he said. "Is that for the city?"

"In this case it would be a federal overseeing position."

"Ah. So did the governor put this in place?"

"He's been looking for somebody for quite a while. It wouldn't be just that city necessarily, but it would be for the state. And, once he found out that you were there and that you were potentially looking for a local job, he immediately asked if you'd be interested."

"Well, I would be interested," he said. "I'm not too sure how I feel about any of it though. And they may not take it kindly when I've got such a bad rep myself in this town."

"Sure, but your past is also what makes you uniquely qualified for the position. You were on the other side growing up there. Now you're on the good side."

"*Hmm.* I certainly have to think about it."

"Well, you have until tomorrow morning. Then he'll be calling you."

"Wow," Kurt said, "that's not exactly giving me a whole lot of time."

"Nope, but life's like that. Besides you've got a wife and a son now, don't you?"

"Whoa, whoa, whoa," he said. "I hardly have that yet."

"What! Then you're not the guy I thought you were," Badger said in a teasing voice. "I've never seen you hesitate."

He snorted. "I want to get it right this time."

"Sometimes you have to go by instincts and figure out what's right as you go along."

"Well, right now, I'm making sure that no asshole comes up this damn trellis to attack her," he said. "My son apparently is staying with his best friend overnight. So I need to make sure that, while he's gone, I capture the asshole planning on giving Laurie Ann a hard time."

"And didn't you say also one of the gang guys knew your

son?"

"Yeah, why?"

"Just want to make sure he doesn't get involved."

"That's not the plan," he said.

"You already know that somehow, sometimes, plans go sideways regardless. So take care and watch your back." With that Badger rang off.

Kurt lay back down beside the dog. He thought about it. A watchdog over law enforcement. Wouldn't that be something? He smiled and realized that, although he had a college education, he hadn't told Laurie Ann about it.

But Badger knew, and he had probably passed that on. Kurt had a degree in behavioral sciences and law enforcement. Maybe, maybe, he had another pathway after all. With a smile on his face, he closed his eyes and fell asleep.

CHAPTER 10

IT WAS HARD to go to sleep. Laurie Ann read a romance book for another hour, even as she half listened to sounds in the house. She heard Kurt on the phone but not the conversation itself. Just lying here and waiting was deadly. When she finally fell asleep, it was already close to midnight. She tossed and turned, and, when she woke again, it was only one a.m. She groaned, pulled the covers up to her neck, rolled over, and fell asleep. She woke up again to find it was two a.m. She knew it would be one of the worst nights she'd had in a long time. She needed sleep in a bad way.

Just then she thought she heard a noise and froze. She couldn't imagine what it could be, and she lay here, straining her ears. She hopped softly out of bed and went to the door. As soon as she opened it, Kurt's voice whispered, "Don't move."

She froze and realized that something was going on and that he already was on top of it. She didn't want to ask, in case the silence was just as important as no movement. She waited and waited, and finally he moved, approached her.

"Go back inside," he said, "and stay. Don't make a sound."

She looked up at him. "Did he come?"

"He is here," Kurt said, in that superquiet voice of his. "I don't want you getting in the middle. Please, go inside and stay."

She nodded, softly closed the door, and sat on the bed. And immediately felt trapped. Nothing quite like a closed door, knowing that all kinds of hell were going on outside, to disturb your peace and quiet. But she didn't know what she could do to help. Then Kurt also had Sabine, which Laurie Ann hadn't seen or heard just now. She frowned. Maybe the dog was also scared. Maybe it had been through too much and was no good as a watchdog anymore.

Her heart immediately melted, thinking about the hardship the dog might have gone through, and, of course, Laurie Ann couldn't do anything about it right now. But, as she sat on the side of her bed, every sound she heard was amplified. Front of the house, back of the house, she heard every little creak, every little whisper, every little groan, as the night air changed temperature.

She got up, grabbed her robe that she had brought into the room with her, put her socks back on to keep her feet warm, and padded over to the window, where she peeked out from behind the curtains. It was dark and stormy. Of course it was. Why couldn't it be a bird-singing night and a clear early dawn? Instead it was cloudy and gray and ugly outside. But as she watched and studied the street, she noted a car she didn't recognize was on the street outside the neighbor's house up one. She pulled out her phone and sent Kurt a text, letting him know. She hoped the sound on his cell was off, in case he was waiting for the intruder.

He responded immediately. **Good, keep an eye on it.**

And, with that, she settled in for the wait. Because, if that guy was waiting for his partner, then she wanted to make sure that he didn't get away either. But she had no way of seeing the license plate. She didn't dare go downstairs, and she couldn't take a useful picture of it from here. She had tried and took several blurry ones but couldn't zoom in close enough. It was an old Oldsmobile, as far as she could see. But that in itself was a unique vehicle. At least they weren't that common in her day and age. As she stayed and waited, she kept listening and turning toward the other rooms to see if she heard anything happening. Every time she found nothing.

Finally she wondered what would happen if she walked over to the door and opened it. As she reached out and touched it, the knob turned under her hand. She slid behind the door. When it opened, a large hairy hand moved inside. She knew it wasn't Kurt. And then all kinds of possibilities came to her, but the head just poked in, looked around at the room, and then popped back out again. She let her breath out ever-so-slowly.

Dear God, what had happened to Kurt? Where was he? What had happened? And she couldn't even breathe, thinking that the stranger was already in the house. How the hell had he gotten in?

And while she tried to figure out what she should do, staring down at the 9-1-1 already keyed in on her phone, she heard sounds outside her door in the hallway—a series of thuds and a growl and another series of thuds and then complete silence. She held her breath, her eyes closed, as she crouched in the corner.

"Laurie Ann, it's okay. Open the door."

She immediately opened the door and bolted into the hallway and stared at him. The intruder was on the ground, and he looked to be unconscious, but Kurt stood tall, barechested, just his jeans on, the dog sitting at his side, looking down at the intruder. Laurie Ann raced forward and threw her arms around Kurt's neck. His arms closed tightly around her, and he just held her close. "It's okay," he whispered. "It's okay."

"Oh, my God," she said, "he came into my room."

"Well, he poked his head in, yes," he said. "Don't worry. He wouldn't have gotten any farther because I was right behind him."

She let out her breath. "I was so scared," she said. "I figured the only way that he would be coming into my room was if something had happened to you."

"No, I was trying to see what he would do, but, as he went through the master bedroom, and then realized that you weren't there, he carried on. And that's why I was trying to see if he would check every room, which he did. He checked your son's room, and then he checked the spare room."

"So he was looking for me?"

"I think so," he said. "I'm not sure what else to make of it."

"But why?" she asked. "I didn't have anything to do with anything."

"Except for those five gang members," he reminded her.

She winced at that. "That's a scary thought," she said. "Nobody really wants to think that a conversation like that will go down a path to this end."

"Exactly," he said. He rolled the stranger over, and she hit the light switch on the wall.

"Oh, my God," she said, "it's one of the five kids from that gang."

"Yep," he said, "it is." He took a photo of the kid and then said, "Shut that light off."

"Why?"

"Because I'll go down and have a little talk with the guy who drove him here." And, with Sabine in tow, Kurt left the intruder securely tied up, and he said, "Don't touch him. If he wakes up, don't even talk to him. The cops are on the way."

She hesitated.

He looked at her and said, "He can't get loose. I promise."

She took in a long slow breath. "That's fine," she said. She walked over to Jeremy's room, picked up his favorite baseball bat, and brought it back with her. "If he wakes up, he's got me to contend with."

Kurt gave a bark of laughter and said, "That's my girl." And he raced downstairs.

LAURIE ANN HAD always been full of grit like that. Kurt loved it. Loved her. Always had. He was just a fool for not even realizing it. It had taken a trip back here for him to figure out what was important in his life, and, now that he found it, he didn't want to lose it. She was just too damn special. And he would do an awful lot to keep her and his son safe and in his life.

He made his way downstairs, and, instead of going out the front door, he went out the back door. Keeping the dog close to his side, loving the fact that she was so well trained that she understood even his rough commands, he let himself out the side gate and headed behind the neighbor's house and down one more. Only her place was fenced; the others just had trees dotting their backyards. And when he got past the car, he stepped out on the front walk and then strolled along the sidewalk casually, as if nothing was on his mind. He checked out the vehicle. It was a dark-colored old Oldsmobile. That, in itself, was interesting because you didn't see too many of them. They were gas guzzlers of the '80s.

As he walked closer, approaching the trunk of the car, he appeared to look at the vehicle, as if it were something unusual—which, in this day and age, it was.

As he stopped to look at it and stepped around it, checking out the tires and the hub cabs, the driver stuck his head out the car window and said, "Keep moving, old man."

He looked his way, smiled at a face in the dark that he couldn't see—and hopefully the driver couldn't make out his face either—and said, "Just admiring the car."

"Yeah, well, don't worry about it," he said.

"Why is that?"

"Because you'll never drive her," he said with a laugh.

Kurt thought he recognized that voice, but he couldn't see the face, still in the shadows. "Hey, no harm done," he said, lifting a hand. "Nice car." Then he stepped back ever-so-slightly and, as he walked about midway along the car, he bent to take a closer look in the interior. And recognized the driver as one of the other kids who had attacked him.

The kid looked at him, recognized him too. "You," he snarled in fury.

"Wow," Kurt said, looking at him.

"What the hell are you doing here?"

Kurt turned, as if innocent, to look around and stopped, stared, and, in a move that surprised the kid entirely, Kurt opened the passenger door, sat inside, and pulled the keys out of the ignition. All before the kid knew it was done.

"Give those back," the kid yelled, hitting and punching

Kurt. Sabine immediately jumped in on top of them, growling at the kid.

"I would stop doing that if I were you," Kurt said.

"Get the fuck out of here. I'll have you arrested for this."

"Oh, is that right?" he said. "Arrested for what? For being the getaway driver as a crime was being committed?"

The guy just stared at him, his eyes huge. "I don't know what you're talking about," he said, his voice squeaking.

"You're already out of your free passes," he said. "It's jail for you next time around."

"You don't know anything about it," he said.

"Yeah, I do," Kurt snapped. "I was once here, and you seem to be determined to follow in my footsteps, but I got out, and you won't. Bad choice to be here tonight."

"I'm just parked, man. I don't have anything to do with nothing."

"You can try telling the cops that," he said.

"What do you mean, *cops?*"

"They are on the way, in case you didn't know."

He shook his head. "I have to get out of here. I can't do no cops."

"Well, you could if you had keys, but you can't, so too bad."

And with that, he stepped back out of the vehicle with the dog. The kid hopped out and said, "Gimme my keys, asshole."

"Nope, I'm not. You're sitting here as part of a crime being committed," he said. "I'm not letting you go anywhere."

"I don't have anything to do with anything. It's not my deal. He asked for a ride, that's all."

"Yeah, and you're sitting here, waiting for him to come

back out, after he kills an innocent woman."

"She's not fucking innocent," he snapped.

"No, maybe not." At that, he heard other neighbors coming out on their doorsteps. "You see? Look at the commotion you're causing."

"I'm not causing anything. Gimme my keys," he roared. He turned to one of the neighbors. "This guy, this asshole, stole my keys."

One of the neighbors came down, half-dressed, a robe around his chest. He looked at Kurt. "Is that true?"

"He's the getaway car for a break-in two houses down—the doctor," he said. "We already caught the intruder and came out looking to see who his partner was. Cops are on the way."

At that, the older man turned and looked at the kid. "Punk-ass kids. They don't even know how to work for a living anymore, and they just want to steal everything."

The kid glared at him. "I don't know what this guy's talking about."

"I don't know about that. You just said something about she's not innocent. Did you go in and attack that poor woman? After all she's done raising her own kid so he becomes a decent citizen of the world. She's a doctor for Christ's sake. Who'll look after you when you end up in the hospital?"

"Nobody'll look after me," he roared. "I'll rule the world. You guys are all assholes and need to die. You're all useless."

The older man looked at the punk and said, "Right, like we haven't heard that before. Petulant bloody kids, that's what it is." He turned to look at Kurt. "You okay with this guy? I want to go in and get a shower and get away from the stench."

"Go for it," he said. "Nice to meet you."

"You with her?"

"Absolutely," he said. "I'll be around a lot now."

"Good," he said, "we don't need any more of these guys." And, with that, he shot the kid another look and said, "Let me know if we need to call more cops," he said.

In the distance they heard the sirens coming closer. The kid started to scream again. "Gimme my keys! Gimme my keys!"

"Nope. Not going to," Kurt said. "So you can either run and I'll come after you and tackle you to the ground," he said, "or you can just sit here and take your punishment, like a man. But, of course, you're not a man," he said. "You're nothing but a punk headed for juvie."

"I'm not going to juvie."

"No, you're probably not," he said. "You'll go to adult court now," he said. "You've mucked up and lost all the goodwill that's available. We'll see how you like jail."

"I'm not going to jail," he said. "No way."

"Yeah, why is that?"

"I've got protection," he said.

"Protection? You mean the guy who is in the hospital?"

"He *was* in the hospital, asshole," he said with a sneer. "You don't know anything."

"No, maybe not," he said, "but I do know that you made the mistake of coming after this woman," he said, "and, for that, I'll make sure you go down."

"You don't know nothing," he said. "I'm not going anywhere."

"It's just a matter of time," he said, "but that's okay. I can see that you don't understand how life really works. Not too smart of you though."

The cops pulled up where they stood, as Kurt talked to the punk. And, sure enough, the detective was in one of the two cars. He got out, glared at Kurt, and then looked at the punk. His eyebrows shot up. "What's this?"

The punk immediately jumped in. "He stole my car keys."

At that, the neighbor came stomping back down. "No, he didn't," he said.

And then the detective faced both of them.

"He's the getaway car for the asshole tied up in Laurie Ann's house," Kurt said, his arms crossed over his chest. "That one broke in her house."

"What the hell for?"

"Well, when I said to this one that he went in to kill an innocent woman, this asshole here jumped in and said she wasn't innocent."

At that, the detective's face turned a thunderous color, and he glared at the kid. "Three strikes and you're out. You know that, right? Now you're involved in a felony crime."

"Nobody got hurt," he snapped. "He was just doing a little R&D for a B&E job."

"Says you." Amos grabbed him and hauled him to the cruiser. Amos looked back at Kurt. "Where's the other guy?"

"In the house still with Laurie Ann," he said.

He studied him for a long moment. "Are you sure about that?"

"I left him tied up and unconscious, and she was sitting there with a baseball bat, standing guard, so I'm pretty sure, yeah," he said, "but you can follow me."

With that, the detective put one of the other officers on the kid that he had in the back of his car, and then he followed Kurt into the house giving the dog a wide berth.

Kurt called out, "Laurie Ann, you up there?"

"I'm here. He's still out cold," she said. "Too damn bad because I'd like to pop him one myself."

He brought the detective upstairs. She glared at him. "You let the kids out, didn't you? And look what they did." The detective rolled the kid over, took one look at his face, and swore. Amos asked, "How badly hurt is he?"

At that, the kid moaned. He opened his eyes and tried to straighten up but fell back because of the ties on his hands and ankles. He glared up at Kurt. "What the hell? What are you doing to me?"

"Well, you broke into this lady's house with all kinds of wonderful intentions," Kurt said. "So we just made sure that you couldn't fulfill any of them."

He shook the cobwebs from his brain, as he turned, finding Laurie Ann and the baseball bat in her hand, his gaze widened. "Shit."

"Yeah, shit," Kurt said. "What do you expect when you come in here and attack a single woman? You gonna get upset when she defends herself?"

"Hey, it was supposed to be a simple job," he said, "just a little payback."

"Really?" he said. "A little payback for what?"

He just shrugged. "For that scene at the parking lot."

"Yeah? Well, how do you feel about a little payback now?" she said in a threatening manner.

He cringed, but he was already tied up and had no place to go.

She looked at the detective and said, "So do you need any more to put this asshole away or will you just let him back out again?"

He shrugged and said, "Again, three strikes out, so this guy will go to jail now."

"Nope, can't," he said. "I'm still a juvie."

"Nope, not now. Not with this kind of a record, you aren't," he said, "You're considered eighteen."

"I'm seventeen," he said quickly.

"Doesn't matter," the detective said. "For something like this, you'll be tried as an adult. Particularly if you came in here with a weapon."

"I didn't," he said, but his response was way too quick.

At that, Kurt looked at her and asked, "Did you check your bedroom?"

"I haven't left him at all," she said.

Kurt motioned to the detective. "While he's lying here, let's go check her room where he came in."

"Hey, I didn't come in with anything," he said. "Anything you find is hers."

"Oh, I don't think so," the detective said. "We can get DNA off anything now."

And the kid started blustering with denials. As they walked into the bedroom, they stopped short because, there on the floor, he had a small hatchet and a handgun and rope in a canvas bag.

"Why would he have dropped those here and then gone from room to room?" Amos asked, pulling on disposable gloves.

"I suspect that he didn't. They were either there for another purpose—or for a second intruder—or he figured that she would be easy to overcome, and then he could come back and deal with her." He paused, looking at Amos. "You could always ask him," he said, "but I think he was just too stupid to realize that he would need them against her."

"Is she the one who captured him?"

"I did," he said. "She saw him out in the backyard earlier in the evening, casing the joint. I believe she texted you that already."

Amos shook his head. "Stupid kids," he said. He walked back into the hallway with the tools all in the bag now. He approached the kid, shook the bag. "Look at these. Rope too."

"Not mine," he said.

"Yeah, well, they're not mine," Laurie Ann said. "And you are so stupid to not even wear gloves. Like the detective said, they can get DNA off anything. So you can BS your way all you want, but you're not getting out of this one now."

"Honest," he said, "I was told to bring them, but I didn't know what to do with them. I've never fired a gun before."

"Ah! So that's why you left it there," the detective said. "Why did you even bring it up?"

"Because I was told to."

"From the boss?"

"Yeah, the boss, and you don't argue with the boss."

"Well, except that the boss is in the hospital," she snapped. "You should be thinking for yourself."

"Naw, he got out already."

She groaned and turned toward the detective. "Seriously?"

Amos just shrugged and said, "The law works in mysterious ways sometimes."

"Depends if you had anything to do with letting them out," she said in an angry voice.

The detective glared back at her.

"Who the hell keeps me safe if you keep letting the animals out?"

"Well, hopefully this guy here," the detective said, motioning at Kurt. Amos looked over at the punk. "And what about the hatchet?"

"Well, I brought that," he confessed.

She stared at him. "What would you do with it?"

"Use it, if you gave me any trouble," he said.

"I'm supposed to just what? Lie here and let you what? Beat me up? Rape me? Is that what you came for?"

He just stared at her and shrugged. "I was supposed to terrify you."

"Well, you succeeded in doing that," she snapped. "What about the rest?"

"If you gave me any resistance," he confessed, "I was supposed to beat you up pretty good."

"Keep me alive, or was that a secondary consideration? Especially considering you thought the hatchet was the tool for the job?"

He didn't give any answer on that. "He just said to make sure that you'd never forget it."

"How nice," she said, her tone faint. She walked to where Kurt stood, Sabine as always at his side. He wrapped an arm around her and tucked her up close. "Don't worry about it," he said. "We've got him now."

"For how long?" she whispered. "Amos let them out last time too."

"It's not that I let them out. We must have enough to hold them," the detective roared.

"And is this now *enough*?"

"Considering he brought a rope and a hatchet and God only knows what else," he said, looking at the bag, "and we haven't even checked him yet. Did you check his pockets?"

Kurt shook his head.

At that, the detective quickly checked the kid's pockets. And what he found there made him even angrier. Handcuffs. What looked like drugs. He lifted the drugs to the guy's face. "If this is a knockout drug," he said, "you're really going down."

The kid started blubbering immediately. "I was just following orders," he said.

"He was supposed to knock me out and then what?" she asked in a horrified voice.

He looked at her, shamefaced. "I was supposed to let them in."

CHAPTER 11

Laurie Ann just couldn't believe what she heard. She looked up at Kurt, but he held her close.

"Nice," Kurt said. "Well, I hope you enjoy jail. I've got some friends over there. I'll make sure I let them know that you're fresh meat," he said in a distant, hard voice.

The kid started crying. "No, no, no. You don't understand. I can't go to jail."

Amos waved the bag and drugs. "Really? And how do you plan to stop it?" the detective asked. "Because this? ... This is beyond a lark now," he said. "This isn't vandalism. This isn't hoodlum bullshit." He dumped the contents of the bag on the kid's belly, causing some pain. "Now you've moved into the big-time. Congrats. An awful lot of jail time is in your future."

And he hauled him to his feet and marched him downstairs. Laurie Ann sank down to the top step and stared as the detective led the punk out of her sight. She felt chills ramping up inside and working through her system. Immediately Kurt sat down, pulled her into his arms, and just held her. And then a wet nose pushed against her neck. She reached up a hand and gently stroked Sabine. "Hey, sweetie. How are you?" The dog nudged her closer, and the three of them just sat, curled up together.

"It's been a really shitty night," she said. "I don't even

know what to think about it. To realize just how close a call I had."

"But luckily you didn't suffer through any of that," he said. "That's the thing to remember. You were smart enough to call somebody who could help you."

"What if I hadn't?" she asked on a whisper. "What if Jeremy were here?" she asked, tilting her head back. "What if he'd woken up? Would they have killed him?"

He didn't say anything, but she could read the answer in his face.

"My God," she said, "I just …" and she fell silent.

"I know," he said. "That level of violence is always shocking. When it's directed at you, it's always horrifying," he said. "But you're okay, and Jeremy wasn't here, and we're making it through this," he said. "Hopefully, with any luck, all of this group will be taken care of."

"I'm scared to hope …"

"Sure, but the cops gave them a chance. They let them out of jail, and they went straight for you," he said. "The judge won't let them out of jail again."

"Really?" she said, "Somehow I'm afraid to believe in that."

"Well, I can make some phone calls, let people know just what's going on here," he said, "and see if we can make sure they don't get out. They don't have an easy future in front of them regardless."

"And right now I really don't care," she said. "They made those choices."

"Just like I made the choices I made a long time ago," he murmured.

She nodded. "And I get that, but you weren't this bad."

"No, but, if I'd stayed, I would have been."

She thought about that for a long moment and then nodded. "I guess once you head down that path, it's hard to back up, isn't it?"

"It is, and you have to get out of it. That's why I had to leave."

"I always knew you had to leave, and I always understood that you felt you had to leave, but I have to admit there were times when I really didn't want you to be the one who was leaving."

"Of course not," he said, "particularly once you found yourself pregnant."

"Pregnant and nowhere to go," she said with a laugh.

"I'll have a talk with those parents of yours," he said.

"Don't bother," she said. "It's a waste of time and energy."

"Well, rejection is a great teacher, isn't it?"

"That's one way to put it," she said. "I really hated them for a long time, and then I realized how much energy it was to maintain that hate. So I let it go, like so much else in my world. I just let it go because I had to focus on the things that I needed to focus on, and that was to maintain my health so I could do right by my son." She added, "Nothing else mattered."

"And that's what is important," he said, "so good for you."

"Maybe," she said, "but now I'm sitting here, tired and exhausted, wondering just how much of any of this is important."

"All of it. All of it. Rarely does anybody in their lifetime come across something like you've had to deal with tonight," he said. "So let's just hope it's over with."

She nodded. "Do we have to go down and deal with the

cops?"

"Oh, yeah," he said. "We'll give statements, and we'll go over the entire scenario and probably have to deal with forensics. I'm not sure."

"Great," she said. "So do you still have your motel room?"

He looked at her in surprise and then nodded.

"So what about us going to your place," she said, "while the cops are all over this place?"

"That's not a bad idea," he said with a smile. "Let's get you a small overnight bag," he said. She quickly packed up a change of clothes, and then they walked downstairs.

The detective stopped, looked at the dog, and asked, "Is she safe?"

"She is. Sabine's also the one who warned me tonight," Kurt said.

The detective nodded. "Well, I'm glad that tonight ended well for you," he said to Laurie Ann. "We need to get your statement. Then you can go someplace while forensics do their stuff in here."

"And you will take a good measure of the place, even though nobody was killed, right?"

"Absolutely," he said.

And this time she believed him. Something a whole lot more concerned and sincere was in his voice.

"I really don't want to end up raped, murdered, or my son killed because nobody cared enough to stop this from happening."

He nodded gently. "We've got them now. They won't be getting out of this one."

"I wonder if a good lawyer would get them out though?" Kurt asked.

"I don't know," Amos said. "Again, we catch them, and somehow they end up back on the streets, no matter how much work we put into it."

And Kurt recognized that same frustration in Amos from before. "Not an easy job," Kurt said.

"No, it isn't," Amos agreed. "About 99 percent of the time, these kids are just bad news and end up dead," he said. "Every once in a while, we find one who escapes the gangs. But it takes us a while to figure out if that was a good thing or not."

And no doubt he was staring at Kurt as he spoke those words.

"In my case, it's a good thing," Kurt said.

The detective just nodded and then motioned to one of his cops. "Go give him your statement and then get out of here," he said. "I'll let you know when we're done."

On that note, Laurie Ann and Kurt headed to the side, where the cops quickly took their statements, and then they were finally free to go. She looked at Kurt and asked, "Where's your truck?"

"I parked it down the road," he said. "I didn't want anybody knowing I would be here."

"Smart move," she said.

"I'm just glad I was here," he said. "I'd hate to think what would have happened if I hadn't been."

"And I don't ever want to think about it again," she said, "because I'll never sleep again if I do."

"Got it," he said with half a smile. The three of them walked in silence as they finally reached his truck, hidden behind an empty house down the block.

They all got into the vehicle, and she watched in amazement as the dog curled up on the seat beside him.

"She's adopted you, hasn't she?"

"You know what? I think she has," he said. "Here I was thinking that I was rescuing her, but now I'm starting to realize she's rescuing me." And, on that cryptic note, he started the engine and drove toward the motel.

KURT WAS STILL shaking inside at how close tonight had been. That's the last ugliness to ever touch her, he swore. She was so sweet, so pure, compared to the life that he'd lived, that it bothered him tremendously to think that anything even close to that dirt could hit her life. And he couldn't even imagine if his son had been there. Jeremy would have tried to protect his mom, and things would have gotten ugly very, very quickly. Not a comforting thought.

When they got to the motel, he brought the two of them inside and looked at the double bed and said, "We'll have to share."

"What? You won't be chivalrous and offer to sleep on the floor now?"

"Tonight we both need sleep," he said. "My nerves and senses will be dulled if I don't."

Immediately her smile fell off her face. "Are we not safe now?"

"We're safer, yes. Are we out of danger? I'm not sure yet," he said. "I want to make sure we have the full headcount of that lovely team locked up before I say yes."

She nodded slowly, and then she walked to the bed, pulled the covers back, stripped down the outer layer of her clothing and laid down in the bed in her bra and panties.

He watched in amazement.

She looked at him, smiled, and said, "We came to sleep, so let's sleep."

Just like that, she curled up on one side of the bed and closed her eyes. He grabbed his phone and sent Badger several messages. It was early in the morning; he wouldn't get them until he woke, but Kurt needed to send off as much of this information as he could. If nothing else, he wanted somebody on his side, just in case more trouble came.

He didn't realize just how much having some friends, decent friends, made a difference in his world. Back then maybe he would have cultivated more friends if he had realized there was a benefit to them. That sounded cold, but it really meant he didn't have the benefit of even understanding what a friend was, not until he had Laurie Ann in his life.

After that, everything had changed but not enough. Yet he also knew, inside his heart, that he hadn't been ready for her. He wasn't good enough. He needed to grow up and change and learn. He just hadn't known what that meant. And now that he did, he was grateful for it. He just wished it could have been in half the time.

Exhausted, making sure that Sabine had a bed on the floor, he curled up in the bed. He was asleep almost instantly.

CHAPTER 12

LAURIE ANN ROLLED over in the night to find herself up against a *body*. She moaned.

Kurt whispered, "It's okay. Go back to sleep."

Her eyes flew open, more awake now, and she stared at him. "How late is it?"

"It's only five in the morning," he said. "Sleep."

She smiled, curled up against him, and said, "I'm really happy that we are together."

"We could have a lot of time together, if we want it," he said.

"I want it," she said instantly. "I just don't want to push you."

"You always don't want to push," he said. "Maybe you should have pushed me a while ago."

"Nope, you had to come on your own," she said. "I have to admit I did look for you for a while, and then I realized you'd moved on, and I just had to live with it."

"I'm sorry," he said gently.

"I know," she said. "I'm just sorrier for the time we missed."

He looked down at her, leaned over, and kissed her gently. "And I don't want to waste any more time," he said. "I was a fool, but I was a young, naive fool. At least I knew what I needed to do to grow up."

"And you did an admirable job of it," she said. "I can't believe it, but you're even taller and bigger than before, even after your accident."

"And yet I lost a lot through that healing process," he said with a smile. "I was quite a bit bigger and heftier before I was injured."

"Well, if it matters," she said, "you can be that way again, but I don't think it matters, does it?"

"Nope, it sure doesn't," he said, chuckling. He wrapped his arm around her and pulled her close.

She could feel his erection between the two of them. She wiggled her hips slightly. "So just how much do you want to make up for lost time?"

"Well, I want to make up in a really bad way," he said, gently rubbing his nose against hers. "But I don't want to push."

"You know what? Everybody warned me that you were this fly-by-night guy who just wanted to get in my pants. But even back then you didn't push it," she said. "I definitely had to force you."

"It was your first time," he said, "and I didn't want you to feel pressured into it."

"Which is also what made you so very different," she said, chuckling. With her arms looped around his neck, she pressed her hips against his. "Besides, it feels very much like I have to force you back into this too."

"Oh, hell, no," he said, "I am totally okay to take the lead on this."

"Are you sure?" she asked in a light tone. "It sounds to me like you're awfully slow."

He let out a bark of laughter, and he leaned over and kissed her like he meant it, like he'd been wanting to since he first saw her again. He could feel their passion immediately sucking him into that spiral that he'd never felt with anybody else since.

When she finally could breathe, she whispered, "I only ever have a kiss like that from you. That is the way it always was with you. I could forget anything and everything as soon as you touched me."

"You think it was any different for me?" he asked. He smiled and kissed her and again, and very quickly it wasn't enough, and little bits of clothing were tossed to the floor. The bedding joined them, and even Sabine sat up and looked at them curiously. When Kurt told her that it was all right and to lie back down again, she chose the pile of bedding and curled up and went to sleep.

Laurie Ann looked at Sabine, smiled, and said, "I guess we already have a ready-made family, don't we?"

"Between Jeremy and Sabine, I would say so," he said with a laugh. He stopped, stared down at her, his fingers tracing the stretch marks on her belly.

She immediately tried to cover them up.

He looked at her in surprise. "Those are not things to be ashamed of," he said, his voice thickening. "To even imagine that my baby was in here." He shook his head. "To see you ripening with my child," he said, "I'm so sorry I missed that."

"Me too," she said. "It was one of the loneliest feelings in the world and yet, at the same time, one of the best because I could feel him inside me, and there was such an amazing bond, such an inherent connection that I never thought to ever have with a human being again," she said. "Pregnancy was a very special emotional and physical relationship with Jeremy before he was even born."

"Have you ever thought about having more?"

"I wanted more. I still want more," she said, "but I don't want to do it alone again."

He looked up, smiled, and murmured, "Well, I was kinda hoping to have a permanent spot in your life."

Her eyes twinkled. "Well, you've always had a permanent spot in my heart," she said, pulling him toward her. "I don't think that's a problem at all."

"You too, huh?"

"Oh, yeah," she whispered, "me too." And she pulled him closer so she could kiss him the way she'd wanted to for so long. A hunger inside her just wouldn't be assuaged any other way but by this man. As she pulled him to her, she cuddled his erection between her thighs and then wrapped one leg up high around his hips and ground herself against him. He shuddered in her arms before rolling over, so he was flat on the bed, and she was high and astride. He looked up at her, smiled, and said, "You always did love to ride."

She chuckled and leaned forward, her fingers busy as she explored his new wounds, scars, stitches, the prosthetic, yet noting his heavier, more muscular, broader build, including his bigger thighs. She marveled at the boy who had become a man. She murmured as she straddled his erection, her hands sliding up and down his shaft. "You've definitely filled out."

He chuckled. "If that's what you call it." And he moaned when her hands turned devilishly tight and slippery. "Don't do that, sweetie. I won't last."

"I won't last at all," she said, "and, after just a short ride here, I plan on neither one of us stopping afterward." And she repositioned herself, ever-so-slowly lowering on his shaft. He groaned and tried to push up higher, but she kept him down, her thighs tight around his hips as she controlled the movement on her own. He lay, shuddering and sweating, on the bed before her, until she was finally seated as deep as she could.

He groaned and whispered, "Dear God, please ride."

"Oh, I'm planning on it." And she slowly lifted and lowered herself, gaining momentum, using his shoulders for balance, as his hands locked onto her hips while she pistoned up and down at a speed just out of control. When she finally cried out, her body twisting as the explosions rippled through her, he gave a shout, flipped her over onto the bed, and drove into her once, twice, three times before he came, surging and groaning above her, his body shaking with his own release, before he finally collapsed on the bed beside her.

She smiled, realizing it was still the same, still as good as ever.

In between gasps, as he tried to regain his breath, he murmured, "What's that smile for?"

"It feels the same," she said, "the same crazy can't-get-enough-of-you feeling."

"Good," he said, "because it's the same for me. Always has been."

"I was worried that all those women would tease you away from me," she said. "Yet you never wandered."

"There was absolutely nothing they could give me that I couldn't get right here," he said, "and I got it even better. I wanted you and only you."

"Same," she whispered. "I'm so glad we found each other back then."

"And I'm so damn glad," he continued, "that we've reconnected now." He pulled her up close and said, "Now go back to sleep."

"Aye, aye, cap'n," she murmured and closed her eyes and

drifted off to sleep.

KURT LAY THERE, watching Laurie Ann sleep, loving to see her so open and honest and yet so trusting in his arms. It was a special feeling, and one he'd forgotten. He'd had a lot of short relationships since her but nothing really serious. He hadn't realized what he had been missing until he had found it again. Life worked in mysterious ways, and he was the first to admit that he didn't understand how any of it worked, but he was just so damn grateful right now that she was here with him.

He closed his eyes and just rested, knowing that the day would start soon enough. He could use a little more sleep, if it was there to come, but he also didn't want anything else bad to happen to them. He just wanted good things for them from now on. If that was possible. And he sure hoped so because it seemed like they had had a rough ride to begin with. And today they would have the family barbecue at the house, if they were allowed back in again.

He frowned, thinking about that, and then pushed it away because it was too early to contact anybody and just drifted off to sleep. He thought he heard a sound, opened his eyes for a moment and then went back under again. Nothing and nobody seemed to be here, and Sabine wasn't worried.

When he next opened his eyes, the sun was a little higher, but a weird stillness was in the air. He frowned, lifted his head, and saw Sabine sitting at the door, her ears up, staring at the door itself. He immediately slipped free of the covers and got up and walked around to where she stood. In a low murmur, he whispered, "What's the matter, girl?"

She just looked up at him, and her tail wagged ever-so-slightly. But there was no give in her stance. He quickly dressed in his boxers and jeans and a T-shirt, put on his socks and shoes. He didn't know if she needed to go out or if something was out there, but he wouldn't take a chance.

At the door, he opened it ever-so-slightly, and she bounded through. He took her around the motel, out back, and she took care of business. He wondered if that's all that she had been after. As they returned to the room, she was ever wary. "Was somebody here last night? What's the matter, girl?" As he reached the door, Sabine stopped and looked down at the parking lot. With these two-story motels, an outside staircase allowed direct access to the rooms.

As he stopped and looked, he couldn't believe the number of vehicles in the parking lot. When they'd gone to bed last night, maybe a half dozen were here. Now there was a good dozen. Was this place that busy? He wasn't at all sure. He moved carefully toward the room, opened the door, checked inside, and noted that Laurie Ann still slept soundly. With that making him feel better, he stepped back outside and studied the layout. Something bothered him, but he couldn't quite figure out what it was.

As long as Laurie Ann was safe inside, he was content to sit out here as a guard. At that thought, the dog growled. Kurt crouched beside her, staring in the direction she was focused on, trying to figure out what was bothering her. He couldn't see anything through the railing. He knew that the dog's sight and other senses were more heightened over humans' senses, and he trusted Sabine's instincts way more than he trusted his. That weird atmosphere was still out here. As he sat down below the railing, he could watch the world slowly wake up.

Just then, he saw a small car parked off to the side that he hadn't previously noticed. As he continued to stare at it, he saw movement inside. As he watched, two of the doors opened. And out came one punk kid, the teen whose shoulder he'd damaged, and another exited the other side of the car—but Kurt had limited visibility on him. Kurt swore, quickly pulled out his phone, and texted the detective. This would be the trouble that he had been half aware was coming at them. This gang couldn't let it go. This was half of the punks, as long as the Reggie kid remained apart from the gang. The other two had been picked up by the cops following the B&E at Laurie Ann's house, but the one in the hospital was here and now had one other gang member with him. That should end it, right? Kurt wasn't so sure, but he hoped so. And, of course, where was the adult who commandeered their loyalty and kept them in the gang?

Kurt had no weapon. But, as he looked down at Sabine, he realized he had her, and she was better than a gun any day. On his hands and knees, he moved to the end of the stairwell, knowing that the gang would come up somewhere close by and head to his room. If they even knew what room he was in. He looked up at the door, glad that he had locked up before coming outside for what should have been a quick pee break for the dog, and then snuck back behind the railing with Sabine.

The two gang members came up quietly. One had a baseball bat, and one had a handgun. And the gun meant they weren't expecting to leave anyone alive. Kurt held his breath and waited, as they came up soundlessly. The dog started to growl. He immediately placed a hand on her muzzle, and she silenced. Kurt recognized the gunman—Slippery Simon. How the hell had he been released?

Kurt had hurt both of these gang members. They had both been in the hospital, then Simon should have been jailed. He must've made bail. Regardless both had obviously either broken out of the hospital or jail or had been released from one or the other. Kurt hadn't seen the other two teens tonight, one being Reggie, but maybe he had decided life was better on the other side of the fence. At least Kurt hoped so. That had been the one Laurie Ann had recognized.

Kurt felt Sabine bristling under his hand, her back going up, her fur puffing out, as she viewed the two men. And he realized that these were the ones who likely had made her life hell. He whispered, "Easy, girl."

She settled ever-so-slightly, but she wanted a piece of these guys, and she wanted it bad. He watched and waited as they came up the last flight, their attention on the motel room door. How were they going to get inside? He wanted to stop them before they got there, but, at the same time, he wasn't sure what their plan entailed. He'd take a bullet gratefully to protect Laurie Ann, but he didn't really want to take the bullet unnecessarily.

If he took the bullet going down with these assholes, that was fine. But any other way? Well, not going to happen. As he watched and considered his options, he figured Sabine would take down the gunman, while Kurt took out the punk with the bat. The pair reached the door and tried the knob; now they were trying to pick the lock. Kurt stood, the dog silently at his side, and he came up behind them. "Can I help you?"

They both spun, stared, and fury crossed the older man's face as he raised the handgun. Sabine immediately jumped, took out his wrist; his loudly crunching bones were hard to miss. He started screaming. But the kid with the baseball bat was already swinging at Kurt. Then tried to swing at the dog. Kurt grabbed the bat, only to have a fist come his way and another one and then another one.

And the fight was on.

Simon was kicking the hell out of Sabine, trying to get free, but the gun had fired widely upward several times before being dropped to the ground harmlessly. Simon was still fighting off the dog, and somehow the baseball bat thumped onto her back end. She might have loosened her grip at that moment, but she obviously bit down again because Simon returned to screaming with a fury.

Nearby doors started to open. Kurt swung the baseball bat and caught the kid hard in the shoulder and then decked him one with a left hook to his face. The kid fell to the concrete walkway and managed to grab the gun and turned and fired at Kurt. He stepped away, Simon taking the bullet in the thigh, Sabine still latched onto his hand.

That newest wound seemed to enrage Simon, and he tried to stay upright.

And now Kurt knew there would be additional trouble.

Kurt grabbed the gun the punk still had, and the two wrestled for it, but he heard Simon coming up behind him. He twisted and turned, trying to keep the kid down. The kid managed to get up to his feet, and they were still fighting with the handgun. Kurt wanted an eye on the dog, but he had to be reassured with her growls and the old guy still screaming behind him. So obviously she remained latched on to Simon. He heard fists and kicks connecting with Sabine, as the dog took a beating too. And he knew that this had to stop, and it had to stop now.

Kurt steadied himself and, with a hard right, he smashed the kid's head hard with an uppercut to the jaw. The teen stopped and stared at Kurt, almost in a comical move, and then he fired the gun again, almost a reflective action. But Kurt now pushed the gun tight against the teen's chest, as they continued to struggle for the gun, just to make sure the gun didn't fire in Kurt's or Sabine's direction.

When another shot was fired, Kurt stepped back, and the kid dropped to the stairwell, a bullet wound to the chest. Kurt looked over at Sabine and immediately stepped up and plowed his fist hard into Simon's head twice. As the guy went down, Kurt immediately stopped Sabine and said, "It's okay, girl. Calm down. Release."

Finally the dog stepped back. He opened the door to their room to see a trembling, terrified Laurie Ann inside. He looked at her, smiled, noted she was dressed, and said, "Get packed."

"I have," she said, "in case we have to run."

"No running," he said, "but call for the police and an ambulance." She nodded.

He looked down to see arterial bleeding from the asshole Simon on the ground in front of them. Kurt had absolutely no hope for the kid beside him. He was already dead, having pulled the trigger that put a bullet through his chest. The other nearby motel doors and neighbors had opened up, and a crowd gathered around them. Kurt checked for a pulse on Simon; he found one, but he was bleeding pretty badly.

"Jesus Christ, did they jump you?" called out one man down the hall.

Kurt nodded. "Yeah. And this one shot him."

"I saw it," one of the men admitted. "They came with a gun and a baseball bat."

"They've been bad news from the start." Kurt tried to clamp down on Simon's bleeding, but he could already see that there was no hope for the older man. Laurie Ann joined him. She quickly bound up the arterial bleeding, doing what she could, but she looked at Kurt and shook her head. Kurt nodded. He didn't say anything.

Today two men had died, and both of them had come to attack them. A solemn group faced the cops when they finally arrived. The detective rushed up the stairs, took one look, and said, "Them again?"

Kurt nodded. "Them again," he said. "I can tell you until I'm blue in the face but the kid shot himself. He pulled the trigger when it was against his chest because we were fighting for control of the gun."

"And I saw it all happen," said one of the other motel guests. "They came here with a baseball bat and a gun. I watched them walk past my door, and I wondered what the hell they were up to. I called the cops, and, next thing I knew, it was chaos out here."

"Yeah, that's about the size of it." The detective said, "Chaos is what they do so well." He shook his head and looked at Kurt. "This is where you've been staying?"

"Yeah, after the attack last night in Laurie Ann's place," he said, "we came here. We needed a place where the dog could go."

"Right, but they found you."

"I'm wondering if they followed us or if somebody else was keeping an eye out. A car is down there," Kurt said, pointing to the small silver one. "It had these two guys in it. For all I know now, there could be more gang members in the parking lot.

Amos nodded. "My men are checking it out."

At that, the silver car backed up and took off out of the parking lot. One of the cops hopped into one of the cruisers and took off after him, blocking his escape. At that, the kid gave up. He was pulled out of the car.

Laurie Ann looked at the scene and sighed sadly. "That's Reggie, the kid who was two years ahead of Jeremy," she said. "I was really hoping, *really* hoping, that he would get free and clear of this."

The detective looked at her and said, "It's pretty hard to get out of the gang once you get in. He's involved in this, and that just won't go down well."

"Well, at least these two were killed," she said, "and not us. So I don't know how you look on it, Amos, but you can't hardly charge Reggie with murder when the two assailants killed themselves."

He nodded. "I don't know what he'll be charged with. That's not my deal," he said. "I haul them in, and then we deal with the outcome afterward. We need to make sure that we have at least enough evidence to prove what went on here." He looked around and said, "Please, everybody, we need statements."

"That's pretty easy," said the one guy, holding up his video camera. "I've got it all on tape."

The detective looked at him in surprise. "Seriously?"

"Yeah, we had also called the cops," he said. And he played back the video, and then the fight was displayed nice and clear. The detective shook his head. "Well, this will go a long way to proving your innocence." He stared at Kurt.

"I *am* innocent," Kurt said drily. "Just think. You know bad guys are out there who have nothing to do with me."

"This guy didn't do anything," protested the guy with the camera. "Obviously this poor woman was in the motel room." He waited a bit, then asked, "What kind of assholes are they?"

"These guys? Bad ones, gang members," the detective said, shaking his head, "but not anymore."

"Wow," the others said.

The cops came and quickly took everybody's statement, some cameras, and contact information. Most of the witnesses were travelers heading in and out of state. By the time they were done, Laurie Ann sat just inside the motel room on the floor, near the open door. She looked up at Kurt, exhausted, black circles under her eyes due to all she'd been through. "Can we leave?"

"They're done with your house now."

One of the men in the crowd asked, "What's wrong with her house?"

At that, Kurt looked up and said, "Two associates of these two assholes attacked Laurie Ann here in her house last night. We came here because forensics was all over it."

"Jesus Christ," the guy said to the cops. "Can't you even protect one single woman?"

The detective flushed. "We're on it."

"Yeah, after they have to save themselves. Twice," the same man said in disgust. With that, he turned and headed back into his own motel room and slammed the door shut. The others in the group muttered equal sentiments.

Kurt smirked, hearing them backing up his side of the story.

The detective studied Kurt. "They are right, you know? I didn't take you at face value, and I didn't see the value in even listening to what you had to say, and I'm sorry." He took a deep breath. "And I allowed that to rule my judgment." He looked over at Laurie Ann. "I'm really glad that you weren't hurt in any of this."

"Me too," she said. "I'm exhausted. I'm worn out. I

don't know if I'll ever sleep again." She added, "All I've had is attacks and intruders. I want to know that this is over, Amos. I want to go home and hug my son and tell him what a great man he is."

"Well, after this," Amos said, "it should be over with. We have the younger two gang members from the B&E already in jail. They'll be charged for the previous two attacks," he said.

"And what about Reggie, the one in the vehicle down there?"

"He'll be charged as well," he said. "The problem now is cleaning up the mess. But that's my problem, not yours."

"Glad to hear that. So I can go back to my house?"

He nodded. "You can check outta here because we'll have forensics in here and do a full investigation. We'll get any other cameras that captured this latest attack, plus what we've got from those witnesses who were observing, and we'll have to get yet more statements from you."

She groaned at that. "Fine," she said, "but I need more sleep, and I have a barbecue to plan."

"Not a problem," Amos said. "Head on home. We'll contact you there."

She looked at Kurt. "You ready to go home?"

He smiled, wrapped an arm around her shoulder, and said, "Absolutely, I'm ready to go home."

She realized just how much that word meant to both of them right now. Because they had spent a lifetime without each other, this was now a perfect time to go home. Together. After they packed up the last of their stuff, they walked down to the truck with Sabine. "Nobody's mentioned the dog, huh?" Laurie Ann asked.

"No," he said, "and I find that interesting too."

"Me too. I mean, it's a good thing. I don't want anybody arguing about who has rights here."

"No, and I'll get something in writing to say that I have the right to keep her."

She smiled. "Thank you for saving me again," she whispered, reaching up to kiss his cheek. And then she walked around to the passenger side of the truck, opened it up, and Sabine immediately hopped in and took her spot between the two of them.

Laurie Ann gently scratched Sabine and said, "You two are saving me again."

Sabine gave a bark that made them both laugh.

CHAPTER 13

"BEFORE WE GO home," Laurie Ann said, "we should stop at the pet store and get some food for her."

"I don't know if anything's open, is it?"

She said, "News alert. All that mess with the cops took a lot of time. It's almost ten."

"Good Lord," he said. He pulled into a pet food store, and they walked in with Sabine on her leash. They quickly bought what they needed and were shortly back in the truck and headed home.

"What about Jeremy?"

"I sent him a text and told him not to come home too early." As they drove up, Jeremy and Frank sat on the front steps. She hopped out of the truck and went to him. She threw her arms around him and gave him a big hug. He looked at her and asked, "What happened, Mom?"

"All kinds of things happened," she said, giving him a misty smile. "But I'm fine. Sabine's fine, and Kurt's fine," she said. "So help us unload, will you? Then we'll go inside and explain what happened."

"Like what though?" he asked. "I haven't been in the house because you told me not to."

She nodded and let them in, pushing open the front door. "We had an intruder last night," she said.

He looked at her in horror.

"Don't worry," she said. "Kurt came. ... I called him early in the afternoon when I saw somebody around the property. Kurt came and laid in wait for him. The guy came back last night, and Kurt caught him."

"Jesus," Jeremy said.

"Don't swear," she said automatically. He just rolled his eyes, and she sighed. "Given what we've been through," she said, "that's the least of my worries."

She walked in, carrying a small bag of dog treats, put them down and then decided where she would put dog food. She opened the closet and motioned at the space on the floor and said, "Put her food in there."

Jeremy dropped the twenty-pound bag, scooted it inside, and asked, "So does that mean we have a dog now?" He looked over at Sabine with interest.

She wandered around the house, looking at him from a distance.

Laurie Ann reached out a hand toward Sabine and explained. "Kids were tormenting Sabine. Those kids were all part of that same gang. She has to decide if you are on the good side or the bad side."

"She'll really think I'm on the bad side?"

"No, but she has to make that judgment on her own, and that depends if she ever has smelled you in the bush tormenting her," she said lightly.

Jeremy looked down at her and said, "You know I love animals, Mom."

She frowned, reached up, gave him a kiss and a big hug. As soon as she stepped back, Sabine was there with one paw up. Laurie Ann crouched and told her son, "Come say hi."

He bent down and accepted the paw shake and said, "Hi, Sabine. How are you doing now?"

She gave a small bark of welcome, her tail wagging like crazy. "You see that?" she said, looking at her son. "That's called acceptance."

"Yeah, acceptance is big," he said, as he looked sideways at Kurt, who leaned against the counter, somewhat close to Frank. Jeremy got up, walked over, reached out a hand, and said, "Hi, apparently you're my father, and I'm really glad to hear that, and thank you very much for saving my mother's life."

"Twice," she said, standing up, keeping a hand on Sabine. "And Sabine did too."

Jeremy frowned, then said, "Okay, sounds like you haven't told us an awful lot of important information here."

"Let me put on some coffee, and also I need food," she said, "and then, yeah, there's a lot to tell you."

By the time they'd all had a small belated breakfast and coffee, the telling took a couple hours. Everyone was getting hungry again, so it was time to fire up the barbecue. About an hour later, when she put the big burgers on the grill, Jeremy looked at her and said, "I'm really glad you're okay, Mom."

She walked over, gave him another big hug, and said, "Me too." She took a deep breath. "And you should also know that your father and I are getting back together again."

He stared at her in shock, looked over at his father, who looked at Jeremy as if waiting for the boom to come down on top of him. "Well, I'm really glad to hear that."

She stopped, stared, and said, "What?"

"Well, as you know, I'm a freshman next year, and I'm thinking of college, and I was afraid—if I picked an out-of-state college and I moved there—that nobody would be here for you. I've still got four years of school before college, but it's been a bit of a worry," he said. "Now he'll be here to look after you."

"News flash. I don't need anybody to look after me," she said, staring at her son in surprise.

"I know, but, Mom, you're lonely," he said, "and I didn't want to leave you all by yourself."

Immediately she felt the tears clogging her throat. She wrapped her arms around Jeremy and held him close. "You've been the best son anybody could ever have," she said, "so thank you for that."

He looked over at his dad and said, "And I hope you'll look after her this time."

"If I had known last time, I would have as well," he said. "But honestly—I know it's hard to understand—but it was a good thing that I left."

Jeremy said, "I understand a little bit. I don't know the whole story, and maybe over time we'll get there," he said, "but she didn't have it easy."

Kurt nodded and reached out a hand to Laurie Ann, and she immediately put her hand in Kurt's. He tugged her close, wrapping an arm around her, and said, "She'll have a much easier time from now on." He added, "Your mother and Sabine."

"Yeah, but do you have a job? Can you look after her? Does she have to work so hard all the time?" Jeremy complained. "And I sure as hell don't want a deadbeat dad," he said. "You need a viable paycheck to support yourself and the dog and Mom."

Laurie Ann stared at her son in shock.

"Not a problem," Kurt said. "I have a phone interview with the governor this morning."

"The governor?" She looked at Kurt in surprise, still

amazed at the change in her son.

"Yeah, they seem to think that I should be a watchdog for law enforcement."

She looked at him, and then she started to laugh. "Oh, my God," she said, "you would be absolutely fantastic at it."

"I don't know," he said. "It's one of those suits-and-desks jobs. Not really my style."

"Does it come with a paycheck?" his son asked suspiciously.

Kurt looked over at Jeremy and gave him a bright smile and said, "A big one."

"Okay then, in that case, maybe it's okay." Then he stopped and said, "But don't you have a record?"

"I had some interactions with the police in my youth, yes. But no convictions, no arrests, or I could have possibly been ineligible for the military," he said. "That's what your mother means when she says I'd be perfect for this position. I know both sides of the law, when it comes to how the law treats people," he said. "I also spent a fair bit of time doing this kind of investigative work in the navy. Not to mention doing missions for and against governments all over the world."

"Maybe you *would* be good at it," Jeremy said in surprise, looking at his father with newfound respect. "The fact is, you saved the dog, and you saved my mom, and that's good enough for me." And, with that, Jeremy held out his hand once more and said, in a very adult voice, "Welcome to the family."

KURT LOOKED AT the proffered hand in shock, surprise, and

admiration. Instantly his hand went out, and he shook his son's hand. "Just so you know, I never stopped loving her."

"Good," he said. "And I hope you suffered for it, just like she did."

Laurie Ann immediately admonished him. "That's enough of that," she said. "We both knew what had to happen. I'm just grateful that we've come back together again."

"I am too, if he makes you happy." His son slanted Kurt a hard gaze. "And if you ever make her unhappy, you know you'll answer to me."

It was all Kurt could do to withhold a smile. He admired his son more in that moment than he ever thought possible. "Got it," he said, "and likewise."

"I'm not the one who'll break her heart."

"There are a lot of ways to break a mother's heart," he said gently, "including bad behavior, … pregnant girlfriends, getting caught by the law for doing something you weren't supposed to, and that's a short list." He shrugged. "I was a pro with all that."

"Well, that's your life. I've chosen a different path," he said. "I'll be an engineer."

"That's right," Laurie Ann said with a bright smile. "I hadn't told Kurt that. It's been your dream since forever."

"It's more than a dream, Mom. Frank and I will both apply to the same universities."

"And, if you want to get in, you will," she said. "You're no slouch in the brains department."

He reached out, gently hugging her. "I got that from you, my mom, the doctor." He looked over at his father, making Kurt smile. "And she did it while raising me."

"I get it," he said. "She's done a phenomenal job."

Frank had been a silent onlooker during all this familial exchange. Frank turned toward Kurt and asked, "But do you have an education?"

Kurt was so impressed with these two teenagers who already had their focus on college. So much suspicion was in Frank's gaze and his tone of voice that Kurt stifled a laugh. "I do, indeed," he said in all seriousness. "I have my master's in political science and law enforcement and negotiation tactics. It's all about the law, from both sides." He watched Laurie Ann's jaw drop. "That's another reason why the watchdog job's being offered to me."

"That's wonderful," she said. "I know you always wanted to get a college education."

"I just never could handle all that blood, guts, and gore that you seemed to thrive on in the medical world."

"No," she said with a dry tone. "You just like inflicting it."

At that, he burst out laughing. "Well, you've got a point, when it comes to the gang in town," he said. "However, it was their bad decision to come after you." He added, "I told you, if they tried to hurt you, they would have to go through me."

At that, the teens just grinned. Kurt looked at the two young men and said, "I don't know about you guys, but I'm hungry."

"Yeah, let's go check the burgers on the barbecue," Jeremy said, "I never could figure out how to make this thing work properly."

Kurt laughed and said, "Let me tell you the intricacies of barbecuing," he said. "That's one of my specialties—and the smoker."

"Cool," his son said. "I'd love to have a smoker here."

CHAPTER 14

LAURIE ANN WATCHED as Kurt and the two young teens, who so badly needed a strong male role model, walked out on the deck and studied the barbecue, as if it held the answers to the universe. And maybe it did. Her world had flipped completely in the last few days. And she couldn't be happier. When the phone rang, and she saw it was her sister, she answered the call.

Sally said, "Hey, sis. Are you okay?"

"Never better," Laurie Ann said. "There's been a ton of changes and a ton of some really unpleasant stuff," she said, "but I do want to tell you that Jeremy and I are fine, that we're okay, and that it's all due to Kurt and to Sabine that we're alive and well right now." She added, "They're here for a barbecue, and everything's going really well."

"And I'm sorry for what I said earlier," her sister said in a small voice. "I'm trying to be open-minded. I guess I'm just scared. I'm scared to lose you."

"You're scared for yourself, and you're scared for me and Jeremy, and I get that. We're not trying to replace you in the family. We would just like to expand the family and bring Jeremy's dad back home again."

"I got it," her sister said, her voice warming up.

"Well, if you got that much," she said, "we have extra burgers on the barbecue. Why don't you come and join us?"

There was a moment's hesitation, then her sister said, "Are you sure?"

And Laurie Ann realized deep down that she'd never been more sure of anything. "Come and meet him," she said. "I promise you'll like him."

"If you're sure?"

"Absolutely," she said, "that's what family is all about."

When she hung up, she walked to the fridge, popped a beer for herself and one for Kurt, and stepped outside to hear the guys talking about the best kinds of smokers. "Make sure we have room for an extra burger on there," she said. "Your aunt's coming over too."

"Oh, perfect. She can meet Dad too."

She looked up at Kurt and caught the big smile on his face at being called *Dad*. "I think that's a very good idea." She handed him a beer.

He looked at it, then her, still smiling hugely. "Thanks, sweetie."

"You're welcome." She looked at the two teens and said, "No, you're not old enough yet."

Both boys just groaned and rolled their eyes.

"I started drinking at fourteen," Kurt said.

"No, you didn't," she said, staring at Kurt. "I think you probably started drinking at twelve."

At that, the younger boys protested, wondering why they couldn't have beers too. Kurt burst out laughing and held out a hand. She placed hers in his and let herself be pulled toward him. "To us," he said, tapping their beer bottles together.

"I'll drink to that," she said and reached up and kissed him gently. Life had never looked brighter. For the first time in a very long time she knew exactly where she wanted to go and who she wanted at her side when she got there.

She lifted her beer bottle and chimed it against his once more. "To all of us. Job well done."

EPILOGUE

TUCKER WILSON WALKED across the property and stared up at the building, then gave a long whistle. "Man, you guys have worked fast," he said. "The new house had gone up like a dream." He looked over at Badger, who stood there with a clipboard, wearing a hardhat. "I didn't think this was your deal?"

"Until all seven of us have houses," Badger said, "it's *our* deal." He glanced at Tucker, noting the lifelike leg under his shorts, and asked, "How's that prosthetic working for you?"

"Well, it's one of Kat's newest prototypes," he said, stretching it out and twisting the ankle. "A waterproof model while on, apparently. I haven't had a chance to try out that part. And, of course, I've got titanium knees and titanium hip joints now," he said. "I'm almost a rebuilt bionic man," he said with a laugh.

"Join the rest of us," Badger said.

"I've got a hankering for heading home though," Tucker said, looking at Badger sideways. "I didn't say anything about it because I didn't want to slow down your progress, and you've been such a great help getting me back on my feet."

"That's what we're here for," he said, "and, if it's time to go home, then it's time to go home. Nobody can tell you when and where, except for yourself."

"Yeah," he said, "it's just one of those things I need to do."

"Any particular reason?"

"My baby sister, Molly, is getting married," he said. "There's just the two of us. She's marrying my old buddy Rodney."

"That's a good reason to go home then," he said. "You thought about work?"

"Well, Rodney's got a construction company, and he wants me to be a foreman."

"Well, you'd do that quite nicely, wouldn't you?"

"Maybe," he said, "but personally I want five acres out in the middle of nowhere and an opportunity to just, … I don't know, maybe raise a few dogs."

"Dogs," Badger said. "You're a dog person?"

He looked at Badger and frowned. "Isn't everybody?"

"Oh no, not everybody is."

"You seem to be running a ton of dog operations through this place. I don't quite understand what that's all about."

"No," he said, "and it isn't always all that clear. But the bottom line is, we're doing a bunch of pro bono work for the War Dog Division."

"I heard about that. You're done though, aren't you?"

"No, they dropped a bunch more files on us. We did the original twelve, and I guess our success has led them to give us a few troublesome cases."

"Great," he said. "Troublesome how?"

"I've got a couple dogs that need rescuing, depending on what quarter of the world you'll be in?" he asked.

"Florida," he said.

"Well, I've got one in Florida, held in a pound, about to

be put to sleep in Miami."

"What? A War Dog?"

"Yes, apparently it attacked a woman."

"And is that confirmed?"

"No. I'm pretty sure nobody gives a shit, and it's just another dog to them," he said sadly. "I've been fighting with them for days."

"Have you got anybody out there to fight on the dog's behalf?"

"No. I'm trying to get them to do DNA testing on the bites, but apparently the woman's refusing."

"Well, that's suspicious as hell."

"She doesn't like dogs," Badger said with a sigh. "So she's not being cooperative."

"Well, Miami isn't exactly my choice," he said. "I don't do huge cities like that. I'm actually from Saint Pete's Beach originally, but, I mean, that's a tourist town. Since my sister's getting married nearby in Tampa though, I'm heading in that direction."

"So no other family?"

He shook his head. "I'm not sure where I'll end up settling. My sister and her soon-to-be husband and his company are based farther out, in a smaller town, where he's doing a couple hundred-unit condo developments."

"So potentially a place where a dog might have a better life?"

"If I have any say about it, yes. Is this one male, female?"

"Female and they're not exactly sure why she turned on and bit her caregiver."

"Aggravation or protecting someone or something," he said immediately.

"Well, that's typical animal behavior. We just don't really know what happened in this case. Nobody's talking. Nobody has any video, and nobody gives a shit. That's the bottom line."

"Yeah, but those dogs have given their lives to the military. The least they deserve is a chance at a decent life."

"She was adopted by the family, and then apparently the parents went on a cruise, and they left her with a daughter, who was attacked."

"And how long was the daughter with the dog?"

"Just a couple weeks."

"*Hmm*," he said. "Well, I can be there first thing tomorrow."

"That would be good," he said, "because I think she's slated to be put down on Friday."

"Two days, counting tomorrow? The dog will die on the same Friday as my sister's rehearsal dinner? That's cutting it really close. Not a whole lot of time."

"Well, I won't be at all upset if you somehow sneak that dog out of lockdown where she is," he said. "We have a little bit of money to help buy her way out, if need be."

"I'll book my flight and head down there right now," he said. "You'll make my sister's day."

"Maybe," he said, "but why don't we make the dog's day and not put her to sleep?"

"What's her name?"

"She's got a big long Latin name, but basically she's Bernadette, and they've shortened it to Bernie."

"That's not a nice name for a beautiful dog," he said.

"She's big, heavily muscled. She's a Malinois with a bit of shepherd thrown in there, typical army breed," he said. "Very well trained and she was a fire dog."

"Well, she should be sniffing out fires then," he said with a frown.

"Wouldn't that be nice," Badger said. "There, you were looking for a dog, ... for a job. Why not that one?"

"It's not exactly construction work."

"Maybe not," he said, "but you have something to do in the interim, if you wanna look for something else."

"Not a bad idea." Just then his phone rang, and he frowned, as he stared down at it. "An SMS message," he said staring at it. "Apparently my soon-to-be brother-in-law has a firebug at one of his condo complexes."

Badger looked at him in delight.

Tucker raised an eyebrow. "You shouldn't look quite so happy about that."

"Maybe not," he said, "but the dog would be perfect to assist on that problem, and we might get a stay on the kill order because of it."

Then Tucker realized what Badger meant. "You got a point there," he said. "I'm on my way. See if you can get us a stay order on the euthanasia."

"Confirm or deny the facts as we know them ASAP," Badger said, "and let me know when you arrive."

"I'll be on the next flight out," he said. "So it all depends on the flight time." He lifted his hand and said, "Nice job for me, by the way."

"If you say so," Badger said. "We're just grateful to have somebody be on the animal's side."

"I'm always on the animal's side," Tucker said. "The real predators in the world are the two-legged ones," he said. "The four-legged ones? Well, their behaviors are simple. It's the humans in the world who you must watch out for."

And, with that, he turned and walked out.

This concludes Book 12 of The K9 Files: Kurt.

Read about Tucker: The K9 Files, Book 13

THE K9 FILES: TUCKER (BOOK #13)

Welcome to the all new K9 Files series reconnecting readers with the unforgettable men from SEALs of Steel in a new series of action packed, page turning romantic suspense that fans have come to expect from USA TODAY Bestselling author Dale Mayer. Pssst... you'll meet other favorite characters from SEALs of Honor and Heroes for Hire too!

Tucker is always ready to fight for the underdog. So when he's offered a mission to save the life of a dog unfairly judged and slated for termination, he can't let her go down without a fight. Plus the dog is in Miami, where his sister lives, and ... no way he can refuse to attend her upcoming wedding.

Addie knows her sister lied about being attacked by the dog, but Addie isn't sure to what extent or how far her sister will go for revenge against an animal she hates. Yet Addie is determined to help the dog who she loves, even if no one else does. Finding a hero to champion her cause isn't part of her plan, but she is quick to realize Tucker's value when she meets him.

Now if only he didn't have a nightmare scenario of his own … one that threatens to take them all down, including the dog.

Find Book 13 here!

To find out more visit Dale Mayer's website.

http://smarturl.it/DMSTucker

Author's Note

Thank you for reading Kurt: The K9 Files, Book 12! If you enjoyed the book, please take a moment and leave a short review.

Dear reader,

I love to hear from readers, and you can contact me at my website: www.dalemayer.com or at my Facebook author page. To be informed of new releases and special offers, sign up for my newsletter or follow me on BookBub. And if you are interested in joining Dale Mayer's Reader Group, here is the Facebook sign up page.
https://smarturl.it/DaleMayerFBGroup

Cheers,
Dale Mayer

Get THREE Free Books Now!

Have you met the SEALS of Honor?

SEALs of Honor Books 1, 2, and 3. Follow the stories of brave, badass warriors who serve their country with honor and love their women to the limits of life and death.

Read Mason, Hawk, and Dane right now for FREE.

Go here and tell me where to send them!
http://smarturl.it/EthanBofB

About the Author

Dale Mayer is a USA Today bestselling author best known for her Psychic Visions and Family Blood Ties series. Her contemporary romances are raw and full of passion and emotion (Second Chances, SKIN), her thrillers will keep you guessing (By Death series), and her romantic comedies will keep you giggling (It's a Dog's Life and Charmin Marvin Romantic Comedy series).

She honors the stories that come to her – and some of them are crazy and break all the rules and cross multiple genres!

To go with her fiction, she also writes nonfiction in many different fields with books available on resume writing, companion gardening and the US mortgage system. She has recently published her Career Essentials Series. All her books are available in print and ebook format.

Connect with Dale Mayer Online

Dale's Website – www.dalemayer.com
Facebook Personal – https://smarturl.it/DaleMayerFacebook
Instagram – https://smarturl.it/DaleMayerInstagram
BookBub – https://smarturl.it/DaleMayerBookbub
Facebook Fan Page – https://smarturl.it/DaleMayerFBFanPage
Goodreads – https://smarturl.it/DaleMayerGoodreads

Also by Dale Mayer

Published Adult Books:

Hathaway House
Aaron, Book 1
Brock, Book 2
Cole, Book 3
Denton, Book 4
Elliot, Book 5
Finn, Book 6
Gregory, Book 7
Heath, Book 8
Iain, Book 9
Jaden, Book 10
Keith, Book 11
Lance, Book 12
Melissa, Book 13
Nash, Book 14
Owen, Book 15
Hathaway House, Books 1–3
Hathaway House, Books 4–6
Hathaway House, Books 7–9

The K9 Files
Ethan, Book 1
Pierce, Book 2
Zane, Book 3

Blaze, Book 4
Lucas, Book 5
Parker, Book 6
Carter, Book 7
Weston, Book 8
Greyson, Book 9
Rowan, Book 10
Caleb, Book 11
Kurt, Book 12
Tucker, Book 13
Harley, Book 14

Lovely Lethal Gardens
Arsenic in the Azaleas, Book 1
Bones in the Begonias, Book 2
Corpse in the Carnations, Book 3
Daggers in the Dahlias, Book 4
Evidence in the Echinacea, Book 5
Footprints in the Ferns, Book 6
Gun in the Gardenias, Book 7
Handcuffs in the Heather, Book 8
Ice Pick in the Ivy, Book 9
Jewels in the Juniper, Book 10
Killer in the Kiwis, Book 11
Lifeless in the Lilies, Book 12
Lovely Lethal Gardens, Books 1–2
Lovely Lethal Gardens, Books 3–4
Lovely Lethal Gardens, Books 5–6
Lovely Lethal Gardens, Books 7–8
Lovely Lethal Gardens, Books 9–10

Psychic Vision Series
Tuesday's Child
Hide 'n Go Seek
Maddy's Floor
Garden of Sorrow
Knock Knock…
Rare Find
Eyes to the Soul
Now You See Her
Shattered
Into the Abyss
Seeds of Malice
Eye of the Falcon
Itsy-Bitsy Spider
Unmasked
Deep Beneath
From the Ashes
Stroke of Death
Ice Maiden
Psychic Visions Books 1–3
Psychic Visions Books 4–6
Psychic Visions Books 7–9

By Death Series
Touched by Death
Haunted by Death
Chilled by Death
By Death Books 1–3

Broken Protocols – Romantic Comedy Series
Cat's Meow
Cat's Pajamas

Cat's Cradle
Cat's Claus
Broken Protocols 1-4

Broken and... Mending
Skin
Scars
Scales (of Justice)
Broken but... Mending 1-3

Glory
Genesis
Tori
Celeste
Glory Trilogy

Biker Blues
Morgan: Biker Blues, Volume 1
Cash: Biker Blues, Volume 2

SEALs of Honor
Mason: SEALs of Honor, Book 1
Hawk: SEALs of Honor, Book 2
Dane: SEALs of Honor, Book 3
Swede: SEALs of Honor, Book 4
Shadow: SEALs of Honor, Book 5
Cooper: SEALs of Honor, Book 6
Markus: SEALs of Honor, Book 7
Evan: SEALs of Honor, Book 8
Mason's Wish: SEALs of Honor, Book 9
Chase: SEALs of Honor, Book 10
Brett: SEALs of Honor, Book 11
Devlin: SEALs of Honor, Book 12

Easton: SEALs of Honor, Book 13
Ryder: SEALs of Honor, Book 14
Macklin: SEALs of Honor, Book 15
Corey: SEALs of Honor, Book 16
Warrick: SEALs of Honor, Book 17
Tanner: SEALs of Honor, Book 18
Jackson: SEALs of Honor, Book 19
Kanen: SEALs of Honor, Book 20
Nelson: SEALs of Honor, Book 21
Taylor: SEALs of Honor, Book 22
Colton: SEALs of Honor, Book 23
Troy: SEALs of Honor, Book 24
Axel: SEALs of Honor, Book 25
Baylor: SEALs of Honor, Book 26
SEALs of Honor, Books 1–3
SEALs of Honor, Books 4–6
SEALs of Honor, Books 7–10
SEALs of Honor, Books 11–13
SEALs of Honor, Books 14–16
SEALs of Honor, Books 17–19
SEALs of Honor, Books 20–22
SEALs of Honor, Books 23–25

Heroes for Hire
Levi's Legend: Heroes for Hire, Book 1
Stone's Surrender: Heroes for Hire, Book 2
Merk's Mistake: Heroes for Hire, Book 3
Rhodes's Reward: Heroes for Hire, Book 4
Flynn's Firecracker: Heroes for Hire, Book 5
Logan's Light: Heroes for Hire, Book 6
Harrison's Heart: Heroes for Hire, Book 7
Saul's Sweetheart: Heroes for Hire, Book 8

Dakota's Delight: Heroes for Hire, Book 9
Michael's Mercy (Part of Sleeper SEAL Series)
Tyson's Treasure: Heroes for Hire, Book 10
Jace's Jewel: Heroes for Hire, Book 11
Rory's Rose: Heroes for Hire, Book 12
Brandon's Bliss: Heroes for Hire, Book 13
Liam's Lily: Heroes for Hire, Book 14
North's Nikki: Heroes for Hire, Book 15
Anders's Angel: Heroes for Hire, Book 16
Reyes's Raina: Heroes for Hire, Book 17
Dezi's Diamond: Heroes for Hire, Book 18
Vince's Vixen: Heroes for Hire, Book 19
Ice's Icing: Heroes for Hire, Book 20
Johan's Joy: Heroes for Hire, Book 21
Galen's Gemma: Heroes for Hire, Book 22
Zack's Zest: Heroes for Hire, Book 23
Bonaparte's Belle: Heroes for Hire, Book 24
Heroes for Hire, Books 1–3
Heroes for Hire, Books 4–6
Heroes for Hire, Books 7–9
Heroes for Hire, Books 10–12
Heroes for Hire, Books 13–15

SEALs of Steel
Badger: SEALs of Steel, Book 1
Erick: SEALs of Steel, Book 2
Cade: SEALs of Steel, Book 3
Talon: SEALs of Steel, Book 4
Laszlo: SEALs of Steel, Book 5
Geir: SEALs of Steel, Book 6
Jager: SEALs of Steel, Book 7
The Final Reveal: SEALs of Steel, Book 8

SEALs of Steel, Books 1–4
SEALs of Steel, Books 5–8
SEALs of Steel, Books 1–8

The Mavericks
Kerrick, Book 1
Griffin, Book 2
Jax, Book 3
Beau, Book 4
Asher, Book 5
Ryker, Book 6
Miles, Book 7
Nico, Book 8
Keane, Book 9
Lennox, Book 10
Gavin, Book 11
Shane, Book 12

Bullard's Battle Series
Ryland's Reach, Book 1
Cain's Cross, Book 2
Eton's Escape, Book 3
Garret's Gambit, Book 4
Kano's Keep, Book 5
Fallon's Flaw, Book 6
Quinn's Quest, Book 7
Bullard's Beauty, Book 8

Collections
Dare to Be You…
Dare to Love…
Dare to be Strong…

RomanceX3

Standalone Novellas
It's a Dog's Life
Riana's Revenge
Second Chances

Published Young Adult Books:

Family Blood Ties Series
Vampire in Denial
Vampire in Distress
Vampire in Design
Vampire in Deceit
Vampire in Defiance
Vampire in Conflict
Vampire in Chaos
Vampire in Crisis
Vampire in Control
Vampire in Charge
Family Blood Ties Set 1–3
Family Blood Ties Set 1–5
Family Blood Ties Set 4–6
Family Blood Ties Set 7–9
Sian's Solution, A Family Blood Ties Series Prequel Novelette

Design series
Dangerous Designs
Deadly Designs
Darkest Designs
Design Series Trilogy

Standalone
In Cassie's Corner
Gem Stone (a Gemma Stone Mystery)
Time Thieves

Published Non-Fiction Books:

Career Essentials
Career Essentials: The Résumé
Career Essentials: The Cover Letter
Career Essentials: The Interview
Career Essentials: 3 in 1

Made in the USA
Monee, IL
18 June 2021